THE REVELATION OF ST. JOHN

NEW TESTAMENT FOR SPIRITUAL READING

VOLUME 25

Edited by

John L. McKenzie, S.J.

THE REVELATION
OF ST. JOHN

Volume 2

EDUARD SCHICK

CROSSROAD · NEW YORK

1981
The Crossroad Publishing Company
575 Lexington Avenue, New York, NY 10022

Originally published as *Die Offenbarung des hl. Johannes 2*
© 1970 by Patmos-Verlag
from the series *Geistliche Schriftlesung*
edited by Wolfgang Trilling
with Karl Hermann Schelke and Heinz Schürmann

English translation © 1971 by Sheed and Ward, Ltd.

Library of Congress Catalog Card Number: 81-68168
ISBN: 0-8245-0134-9

OUTLINE

THE KERNEL SECTION
OF THE APOCALYPTIC PROPHECY
(12:1—14:5)

Introductory Vision (12:1-17)

The new cycle of prophecy (cf. 10:11), which unfolds the content of the seventh trumpet in individual images, begins with the disclosure of the final background before which alone the spiritual combats and the bloody battles as well as the positive developments and salvific events in world history can be correctly classified and understood. The actual driving forces of history as of the involvement to which the Church is exposed in it are highlighted in sharp profile in the introductory vision. The interpretation of reality offered here contrasts with the widely accepted view of today that the world is occluded and is its own explanation. "The Seer however is made familiar with its uncanny backyards and deep, dark lanes which are simply not noted in most of the philosophical city maps because they are not allowed to exist."

In order to disclose the understanding of the Church in the world the foundation vision comes to speak at first of the innermost secret of the Church and her historical role which results from this. To explain the experience which the Church has in and with the world, the role of Satan in world history as working contrary to her nature and aim must be clarified. The mystery of the painful combat imposed on her is thereby explained in its final origins (12:1-6) and its outcome disclosed (12:7-12). That, and how, the Church is kept safe through the humanly speaking hopeless situation of the final time, and is liberated from the mortal threat of the antichrist (12:18—13:18), is assured here expressly at the end of the vision (12:13-17). The prophetic passages which are then still to come (14:1—20:10) delineate the gradual weakening of the forces hostile to God and their final exclusion from God's creation for ever.

The Two Portents in Heaven (12 : 1–6)

[1]And a great portent appeared in heaven, a woman clothed with the sun, with the moon under her feet, and on her head a crown of twelve stars; [2]she was with child and she cried out in her pangs of birth, in anguish for delivery.

Everything in the world, even what is perverse, can only be understood from God; hence the vision which aims to explain in its origins the conflict between the Church of God and the spirit and the power of the world by the essential turning point of world history, begins with the incarnation of his Son. In him the creator has embraced his world, which is in a sorry state, as saviour; thereby the final time, in which her reconstruction to perfection is advanced, has begun; the entire history of mankind both of fall and redemption is captured with masterly strokes in the austerely etched pictures of the twelfth chapter.

In two great portents, the contrast between the woman and the dragon, the secret of history, is unfolded, the knowledge of which is necessary for understanding and endurance, especially of the final time before the end. First the gaze is turned to the Redeemer of the world so that the terrifying sight of the destructive power of the antichrist might be better endured.

The first " portent," that is, a symbolic apparition, is seen by the Seer on the background of the starry skies as the figure of a woman in shining light. All the sources of light in the universe contribute; the sun is her garment, the moon her pedestal and twelve stars form the crown on her head. In sharp contrast to this supernatural glory, the Seer hears the woman crying out with pain; he notices that she is with child and suffers birthpangs.

³*And another portent appeared in heaven; behold, a great red dragon, with seven heads and ten horns, and seven diadems upon his heads. ⁴His tail swept down a third of the stars of heaven, and cast them to the earth. And the dragon stood before the woman who was about to bear a child, that he might devour her child when she brought it forth;*

The second " portent " is characterized by color, monstrous size and destructive activity as a being from the abyss which destroys order and loves chaos and darkness; the dragon is God's adversary who devastates his world and seeks to negate his salvific intentions; later it is expressly stated that he symbolizes Satan (12:9). The entire shape of the monster, for whose portraiture elements from the Book of Daniel (Dan. 7:7; 8:10) are utilized, reveals, moreover, the miscarried attempt at being God; his appearance therefore presents itself as a grotesquely distorted imitation of the " Lamb," the true Lord of world history; the seven eyes, symbols of God's Spirit (5:6), have become seven heads, the " seven horns " (5:6) have increased into ten, and the " many diadems " (19:12) appear here as seven crowns. The incongruity and pretentiousness of this figure make clear that here imitation has turned into perversion and that the arrogated divine power is channelled into protest against God's power and its negation. But the warning signs are not to be ignored: Satan is truly very strong (" ten horns "), he possesses sovereign power (" seven crowns ")—hence Jesus calls him the " ruler of this world " (Jn. 12:31; 14:30; 16:11; cf. Mt. 4:8f.)—and is animated by an uncontrollable destructive wrath ("a third of the stars" are swept down by him). Thus this monstrosity stands before the luminous figure of the defenseless woman to devour her child as soon as it is born.

⁵she brought forth a male child, one who is to rule all the nations with a rod of iron, but her child was caught up to God and to his throne; . . .

The child is born; it is a boy whose identity and mission are noted with a quotation from the psalm of the Messiah-king (Ps. 2:9); according to this the new-born child is the promised Messiah appointed by God to be ruler over all the nations, that is, God's ambassador who is to cast out the "ruler of this world" (Jn. 12:31) from his present position of power. That would explain the tense preparedness with which the dragon awaits the birth, and the zeal, issuing from an instinct of self-preservation, to clear his foe out of the way right at the start. All the circumstances are clearly favorable for his success: a new-born child, expression of utter helplessness, on the one hand; on the other, the powerful, wild dragon fighting for his survival. Nevertheless, the most unexpected happens: the Almighty God himself intervenes; he rescues the child and makes him into his co-ruler on his throne. By this remarkable foreshortening of the life-story of Jesus to the beginning and the end of his Messianic career what is essential in his person and life work is strikingly brought to the foreground. Basically, for those who know, all the stations of Jesus' life and activity are comprehended and brought to mind in this symbolization of the mystery of the incarnation, beginning with the flight into Egypt, the temptation in the wilderness, the casting out of demons to the persecution on the part of the Jewish authorities and the crucifixion on Golgotha on the one hand; and on the other, the death on the cross, the beginning of his exaltation (Jn. 2:31f.) by way of the resurrection to the ascension into heaven. Precisely by means of this foreshortening of perspective, an insight important to Revelation's motif of encouragement is brought to the foreground, expressed by St. Paul in the words: " God chose what is weak in the world to shame the strong, God chose . . . even things that are not, to bring to nothing things that are " (1 Cor. 1:27). This weak human child snatched from the jaws of Satan by being caught up to God's throne puts into proper perspective all assaults which he overcame in his life as well as his apparent defeats.

6. . . . and the woman fled into the wilderness, where she has a place prepared by God, in which to be nourished for one thousand two hundred and sixty days.

It will be no different with the Church, who seems to be delivered up to the superior power of Satan, like the helpless woman to the dragon, for better or for worse. God takes charge of her as he does of his Anointed, hence all the great possibilities of her superior opponent are to be frustrated. Although her way on earth is like the flight of the first chosen people of God from the power of the Pharaoh and its long journey through the wilderness she will like Israel be protected on her dangerous path and brought to her goal. He cared for her during the entire time of her need and peril; twelve hundred and sixty days is the epoch of the occupation of Jerusalem by the heathen (11:2), of the appearance of the two witnesses (11:3) and of the reign of the antichrist (13:5).

The last sentence of the extraordinary image leaves no doubt how John himself understood the " apocalyptic woman." Into the drawing of the woman, as well as of the dragon, there may have entered ideas from heathen myths, especially of astromythological origins, or philosophical speculations of the later Old Testament writings may have contributed, or the prophetic comparisons of Israel as a woman wedded to Yahweh may have stood as a model, all these ideas John could use if they helped to make his allegorical utterances intelligible to those for whom he first intended them.

The woman is the mother of the Messiah, but, at least to begin with, not the historically unique person of the virgin Mary but the Old Testament people of the covenant imagined as a collective person who was called to give the world the Messiah of God as its redeemer (cf. Rom. 9:5). Thus the individual elements find a meaningful interpretation: the twelve stars of the diadem refer to the twelve tribes; already the prophets have compared the story of Israel on its way to its special calling with birthpangs (cf. Is. 66:7–9; Mic. 4:9f.), in the later Rabbinical literature the expression "Messianic pangs" became a standing formula. But in the further unfolding of our vision the mother of the Messiah grows beyond the framework of the people of Israel when after the birth she, persecuted, flees into the wilderness where God prepares a place for her during the time of the antichrist; the Old Testament people of salvation have been transformed into those of the New Testament, the Church of Jesus Christ; both together form an organic unit in the history of salvation (cf. the connection between the twelve tribes and the twelve apostles in the symbolic description of the heavenly Jerusalem in 21:12–14).

A further metamorphosis in the unfolding of the image must not be ignored either: the luminous form on the firmament changes into the poor persecuted woman in the wilderness. Idea and reality, supernatural essence and earthly appearance, eternal election and transitory destiny of the Church—all this is caught up in the few strokes of this changing image. Probably in the background of this image the influence of another late Jewish conception has also made itself felt, one which can be found especially in the Jewish apocalyptic writings: all the benefits of salvation of the Messianic epoch are already present with God in perfect form in heaven before their earthly realization, thus also the salvation community of the final time as " heavenly " or " higher Jerusalem," an idea which is also found in New Testament writings (Gal. 4:26; Heb. 12:22; Rev. 21:2ff.). Thus this image of the woman, " one of the most powerful and deepest symbols of Revelation " (R. Gutzwiller), represents in spare strokes the people of God in its widest extension, according to its eternal idea and supernatural essence as well as its historical appearance and experience. The reference to Mary, the Mother of God, is also based on the typological relation which according to an old theological tradition of the Church exists between Mary and the Church.

The Fall of the Dragon (12 : 7–12)

[7]*Now war arose in heaven, Michael and his angels fighting against the dragon; and the dragon and his angels fought, . . .*

The image is a continuation of the first inasmuch as it appends on a supernatural plane the reason for the wrath as well as the impotence of the dragon; moreover, in this vision the existence of the power hostile to God within his creation is explained in the story of its source. Whatever results as personally significant for the faithful from these factual assertions is finally explained by a celestial voice.

The first image delineated Satan's attempt to impede the redemptive act of God; the second image throws a light on the hopeless consequences which have resulted for the adversary of God from Christ's work of redemption. This is symbolically performed for the Seer in a battle scene which takes place in heaven.

The idea of a fall which the rebellious spirits experienced before time began, when they were defeated by the angels who remained loyal in the service of God, stands behind these portrayals. To this extent an explanation concerning the origin of evil is also contained in their substrata; evil is present in the world, not as an external principle but in the shape of originally good angels, powerful spirits who fell away from God and were therefore cast out. Moreover, in the story of the temptation of the first human couple the reason for the angel's fall is hinted at when the serpent (cf. v. 9) tried to inspire Eve with its own dream-wish: " You will be like God " (Gen. 3:5); the same is also suggested in the name of the leader of the good angels, Michael (" Who is like God?")—which is after all the battle cry of these angels. The two contrasting slogans in the combat of the pure spirits projected into the world of men explain fundamentally all conflicts in the history of man as well as in the life of the individual.

In the first place, however, John is shown in this vision that the redemptive act of Christ rendered the Devil powerless which, moreover, Jesus himself expressed with the same image (Lk. 10:18).

8but they were defeated and there was no longer any place for them in heaven. 9And the great dragon was thrown down, the ancient serpent, who is called the Devil and Satan, the deceiver of the whole world—he was thrown down to earth, and his angels were thrown down with him.

The battle itself need not be filled in by the vision because it is from the outset just as hopeless as the attempt of the dragon described in the first image (12:5); it suffices to announce the defeat of Satan and to record the consequences which resulted from it. For the Devil himself and his supporters it meant the final and irreversible fall—three times in one sentence the words " thrown down " are repeated like a cry of victory. His power is broken; what he has lost thereby is, to begin with, noted in the three names which are applied to him. He is the " ancient serpent," who succeeded in leading our first parents astray (cf. Gen. 3:1–7); his sly, cunning behavior has merited him from the lips of Jesus the characterization " father of lies," and in view of the tragic consequences for the human race (Gen. 3:2–24), the other, " a murderer from the beginning " (Jn. 8:44). The second name, " Devil," in English borrowed from the Greek, originally meant something like " slanderer," " maker of disorder " (cf. v. 10); all disorder in the world, all misunderstandings and enmities among men go back to him. The third name, " Satan," is Hebrew and means adversary, opponent of God. His intentions and endeavors among men are in conclusion summarized in the designation: the deceiver of the whole world (cf. Mt. 24:23f.).

[10a]And I heard a loud voice in heaven, saying, Now the salvation and the power and the kingdom of our God and the authority of his Christ have come, . . .

As it happened so far with every salvation event this one too is celebrated in heaven with a hymn and thereby its meaning is unfolded. This time it occurs in a solo which is rendered by a representative of redeemed humanity—probably one of the " elders " (cf. 4:4)—in the name of all (" our brethren "). He announces the turning point in the history of mankind which has occurred with the sacrificial death of the Messiah and Son of God (" the Lamb "). With him the breakthrough battle has been fought which assured the victory of Christ; the time of salvation in God's kingdom has " dawned " which although not consummated can never be reversed and of necessity moves towards its completion.

[10b]. . . *for the accuser of our brethren has been thrown down, who accuses them day and night before our God.* [11]*And they have conquered him by the blood of the Lamb and by the word of their testimony, for they loved not their lives even unto death.* [12]*Rejoice then, O heaven and you that dwell therein! But woe to you, O earth and sea, for the devil has come down to you in great wrath, because he knows that his time is short!*

For redeemed mankind this means that the just claim of Satan, which originates from the mistaken decision of the first human couple, which Satan incessantly (" day and night ") asserts before God, is now lifted (cf. Rom. 8: 33); the relationship of bondage has now expired. Not merely legally, but also practically a change has occurred for mankind through the redemptive act of Christ. " By the blood of the Lamb," with the help of the grace which Jesus Christ has earned for them on the cross they themselves have received the ability to master evil; the victory of Christ is victory for all. The clearest and most convincing proof of this is demonstrated by Christians in the attitude of superiority with which they seal their loyalty to the faith by death. By virtue of the grace of Christ, no demand not even the extreme of bloody martyrdom means an overstrain. To impart such an unconditional consciousness of superiority is the main purpose of this vision and this purpose is effective down to the formulation when in the form of the prophetic perfect (" they have conquered ") even the individual victories in every Christian life are asserted not only as possible but as already actual. The reason why it means so much to the Seer to build up such an unshakeable certainty in the conviction of his readers is made comprehensible in the concluding word of the celestial voice. The " woe " leads over to the next image and looks even beyond it to the horrifying images of the following chapter which shows the antichrist at work. At the roots of Satan's wrath, the terrible discharge of which is depicted here, gnaws the despair of one who knows his destiny is already sealed and sees the moment already near at hand when he will be finally banished out of this world into the " bottomless pit "; as does Satan himself, so also the prophet regards the time till then as " short " when measured against eternity.

The Persecution of the Woman and Her Rescue (12 : 13-17)

[13]And when the dragon saw that he had been thrown down to earth, he pursued the woman who had borne the male child. [14]But the woman was given the two wings of the great eagle that she might fly from the serpent into the wilderness, to the place where she is to be nourished for a time, and times, and half a time.

The second image has revealed what power and what intentions are at the root of the bitter experiences of the persecuted Church on earth: creaturely arrogance in the world of spirits which sought to usurp the sovereignty of the creator, and the fall which followed this defection. There is no repentance for Satan and his cohorts and hence no return. A failure as a rebel against God, and obdurate in his protest he utilizes the last possibilities which are still left to him, at least to continue to demonstrate his impotent rebellion among men. Thus he exploits all means in order to disrupt, or if possible, to destroy the kingdom of God established in the world by the redemption. Thus the war in heaven continues on an earthly level and is here directed above all against the Church which at the end of the first image already appeared under the sign of the woman fleeing from him. The third image is immediately linked to this (v. 6). The beginning of the first sentence almost sounds like irony, for the fallen dragon seems to need some time to grasp his situation; he needs first to recover his senses before he takes up the pursuit of the woman. But this undertaking is just as hopeless as the first; this is then depicted symbolically.

In a wonderful image, which is drawn with the help of the account of the rescue of Israel from the Pharaoh and her preservation during the trek in the wilderness (Ex. 19:4; Deut. 32:10–12), the promise of Jesus concerning the indestructibility of the Church is once more illustrated (Mt. 16:18), having been already symbolically depicted in the image of the temple-measuring (11:1f.), as well as his repeated prediction of the persecution of his disciples (Mt. 5:10–12; 10:23; 23:34; Jn. 15:20). The redeemed people of God will during the entire time of their ordeal (" three and a half years ") experience the same supernatural help which God has bestowed on them from the beginning; as an eagle who takes his young on his back in flight in order to save them, God has revealed himself to Israel (cf. Deut. 32:11); just so will he show himself to his Church especially in the perils of the last onslaught of his adversary.

[15]*The serpent poured water like a river out of his mouth after the woman, to sweep her away with the flood.*

In the scene of pursuit, the " serpent " (the Devil) turns into a sea monster which spews masses of water out of its mouth after the woman, as massive as a river to sweep her away and be drowned. Ezekiel in one place compared the Pharaoh who wanted to destroy Israel at the Red Sea after the exodus to a " dragon in the sea " (Ezek. 32:2; cf. also 29:3); besides this stimulus from the Old Testament, there may have been mythical traditions from the heathen world which helped to form this daring image.

16But the earth came to the help of the woman, and the earth opened its mouth and swallowed the river which the dragon had poured from its mouth.

That the earth comes here to the woman's rescue would indicate that God does not merely by extraordinary means secure the existence of his Church; the whole world is his property, forces of nature as well as the spiritual forces in mankind can be set in motion to achieve his aims and so let the rulers of this world feel who is the " sovereign Lord."

17Then the dragon was angry with the woman, and went off to make war on the rest of her offspring, on those who keep the commandments of God and bear testimony to Jesus.

The Church is secure in God's wonderful help; but that in no way means that she has peace in the world. Although safe against destruction by Satan, he tries incessantly by persecuting her members to impair the kingdom of God and put it in jeopardy.

The faithful are characterized twice here: they too are off-spring of the woman who gave birth to the Messiah, the Son of God, and they are recognizable in the world on account of their faith whereby they " bear testimony to Jesus " and by their behavior in keeping the commandments of God. They have inherited the witness for which he went to his death; they are now his witnesses (Acts 1:8; 10:49; 13:31) and ready for this task with a fidelity unto death. Antipas (2:13) was therefore credited by Christ the " faithful witness " (1:5; 3:14) with the same honorary title: " my faithful witness " (2:13). Satan's persecution of individual believers achieves, in the case of those who are so truly, only the opposite to what the Devil intends; they crown their Christianity with its final glory in the probation of surrender to God to the extreme of self-immolation in death and thereby manifest the greatest possible likeness to the witness Jesus, their brother. The furious rage of Satan therefore serves towards the revitalization and glorification of the Church of God, the inner growth of the kingdom of God on earth.

This introductory vision contains an abundance of deep theological ideas: The Church in this world; her real secret is invisible, she lives under the protection of the Almighty by the grace of what her master had done and suffered for her in his earthly life. In the place of the accuser who after the original fall had accused mankind incessantly before God (12:10) now stands the redeemer who, raised to the throne of the sovereign Lord, appears there on their behalf (cf. Heb. 9:24). The Church is our mother and Christ is our brother (12:17; cf. Heb. 2:10–18). As he himself had experienced and endured, all who hold part with him must prepare themselves and learn how to live under the wrath of the dragon. A church, no longer hated and persecuted, should seriously ask herself whether she still is the Church of Christ.

Having indicated that the persecution is to be expected as a matter of course, which is the chief declaration of the last sentence, the image then leads on to the following vision which displays the war of the dragon against the people of God on earth in its greatest intensity under the antichrist.

The Two Beasts: The Mortal Threat to the Church (12:18—13:18)

The First Beast, the Antichrist (12 : 18—13 : 10)

The images of the introductory vision (12: 1–17) have disclosed the background and final *raison d'être* of a Church history manifesting a profusion of catastrophes in this world; they were especially intended to elucidate and prepare for the following startling scenes of the final phase which concludes in the return of the Lord and the judgment of the world.

The image of the two beasts is among the most horrifying and gruesome things that the writer of Revelation has to portray. He therefore does not want to contemplate it in isolation but in the light which the introductory vision (12: 1–17) throws on the intimidating sketch; then despite all the horror of the external events the decisive knowledge remains lodged unclouded in the mind that here we have only the despairing skirmishes of a retreating enemy who is already certain of his destruction; of course it is precisely the despair arising from this which determines his unbounded and uninhibited commitment to hostility.

By taking note of a certain correspondence, which lies at the root of the portrayal, it will be easier to understand: the image which imparts to us the revelation of God is contrasted with its negative counter-image, the negating imitation of God in Satan. God's purpose for the world and the corresponding work wrought on and in it—beginning with the creation via redemption to the consummation of the world—also reveals what the intentions of his antagonist are, and what means he will use for his purpose. Just as God sent his Messiah from heaven to redeem mankind so Satan resurrects a " world redeemer " out of hell to " redeem " mankind from God and his Christ. In the image of a negative imitation of the Messiah of God by the employment of the " antichrist " and his aids, a contrary course in opposition to the history of salvation is unfolded in world history; Satan, who did not succeed in thwarting the work of redemption from the beginning (12:5), now tries to make it senseless, and useless in its final outcome, by taking measures to influence mankind (12:17). The interference of this power hostile to God will accompany the Church of Christ like a dark shadow on its way through history till the return of her Lord.

The adversary of God learns thereby from his successes as well as his failures; the plans which he contrives and the arrangements he makes become through experience more deliberate and more crafty until finally he summarizes all this and incarnates it in a historical phenomenon, the person and work of the antichrist. The combination of power and spirit, of compulsion by external force and sly persuasion by seductive propaganda, all these means employed at the greatest possible intensity characterizes the last despairing attempt of the " god of this world " (2 Cor. 4:4) to remain at the helm in world history.

18*And he stood on the sand of the sea.*

1*And I saw a beast rising out of the sea with ten horns and seven heads, with ten diadems upon its horns and a blasphemous name upon its heads.* 2*And the beast that I saw was like a leopard, its feet were like a bear's, and its mouth was like a lion's mouth. And to it the dragon gave his power and his throne and great authority.* 3a*One of its heads seemed to have a mortal wound, but its mortal wound was healed, . . .*

The dragon, the symbol of Satan (12:3) earlier introduced as a water spewing sea monster (12:15), raises out of his element the sea—a last reminder of the pre-terrestrial chaos (cf. Gen. 1:1f.; 2 Pet. 3:5f.; Acts 21:1)—an assistant; a creature from the bottomless pit (cf. 11:7), a malformed, bestial colossus rises out of the water. His upper part is like a mirror image of the dragon (12 : 3) except that the diadems, the symbols of power, have been increased to ten; a hint that in him Satan employs the entire fullness of his power. The Seer is not so much concerned with the description itself as with the intimations he would like to make through the individual features about the nature and function of the beast. High intelligence (" seven heads "), great strength (" ten horns ") and sovereign power (" ten diadems ") are combined in it as in its archetype Satan who makes his appearance in it. That it represents God's adversary is made clear by the names which are on its heads; they are titles of majesty with which it pretends to be God.

One may infer from the further description of the monster, that in this image the Seer has fused into one the four beasts which Daniel was shown in a vision (Dan. 7 : 2–7); the four beasts symbolize the four earthly kingdoms in Daniel (Dan. 7 : 17–25); in the case of the fourth the prophet expressly gives prominence to the difference in the nature of his power (Dan. 7 : 24), and the anti-theistic character of his doings (Dan. 7 : 25), also his warning against the " saints " (cf. 13 : 7) is expressly mentioned twice (Dan. 7 : 1. 25). If John utilizes for his portrait these symbolic figures of four earthly kingdoms in Daniel and condenses them into one beast then this implies surely that he sees the antichrist to begin with as the wielder of political power who employs all his power for the purpose of removing from the earth the last remains of God's kingdom and to assist God's adversary towards the attainment of absolute authority over the world and mankind.

That the endeavors of the beast truly reach their summit in this, indeed, that this is the meaning of its entire existence, is expressly highlighted by the act of delegation whereby Satan transfers his power to the beast. Moreover, in this detail of the delegation of power, imitation and parallelism with the Messiah of God become clearly evident (cf. Mt. 28:18; Jn. 17:2) insofar as the limits of power seem similarly extended as that which Christ asserts of himself in his life-time (Jn. 10:17f.) and has put to the test in his resurrection (2:8). That the antichrist himself is capable of representing the resurrection of Christ in a Satanic perversion has an especially convincing effect on the people, which is twice more stressed later on (13:12. 14); they follow the beast with astonishment as if it were a living miracle.

In the symbol of the continuous regeneration of mortal wounds and the ability of the beast to revitalize itself there seems to be expressed first and foremost that the anti-theistic power of the antichrist will be continuously present in history after Christ; when one of its holders leaves the scene ("mortal wound") it does not perish itself; its enduring presence gives the impression of invincibility and the illusion of eternity.

[3b]. . . *and the whole earth followed the beast with wonder.* [4]*Men worshipped the Dragon for he has given his authority to the beast, and they worshipped the beast, saying, Who is like the beast, and who can fight against it?*

This power which pretends to be absolute and total achieves the intended effect on mankind; all men acknowledge the beast and him who has given it authority as a divine being. The religious cry: "Who is like the beast . . ." signifies an apotheosis of the authority and of its holders. The dragon is acknowledged as its true foundation; but since he belongs to an extra-worldly order and remains invisible himself the divine honor acknowledged as due to him is offered to the beast as the reflection of his nature whose connection with the dragon is unmistakably delineated in analogy with the relationship between God and Christ who is characterized in Scriptures as "reflecting the glory of God and bearing the very stamp of his nature" (Heb. 1:3). Thus a religion of the beast is established in an antagonistic correspondence to the religion of Christ; in place of the worship of God and his Christ there appears the cult of the Devil and his ambassador in a blasphemous mimicry.

[5]*And the beast was given a mouth uttering haughty and blasphemous words, and it was allowed to exercise authority for forty-two months; . . .*

Before the efficiency of the beast is delineated, the instrument, which it utilizes most of all, its mouth is referred to. The first thing mentioned about it is that it "was given"; here God is understood (cf. also Jn. 19:11) as the logical subject of this in Revelation oft-repeated passive form (e.g., 6:2. 4. 8. 11; 7:2; etc.), because all that exists owes its equipment and potentialities to him. Even when creatures use their powers against their creator it can only happen with his permission; the latter is expressly underlined as above (11:2) by the detail of a definitely circumscribed time-limit for the possible influence of the beast, namely, the apocalyptic time-measure of evil (cf. 11:2).

[6]. . . *it opened its mouth to utter blasphemies against God, blaspheming his name and his dwelling, that is, those who dwell in heaven.* [7a]*Also it was allowed to make war on the saints and to conquer them.*

As an accomplished speaker the beast knows how to arouse attention and make an impression with "haughty words"; but its captivating, fascinating eloquence is used exclusively for blasphemy. The blasphemous names on its head (13:1) which are to characterize its nature are now confirmed by its words; his eloquence is against God, against everything that belongs to him and against all who take sides with him in heaven and on earth. Besides words, the beast can also fight God's faithful on earth with deeds; so it instigates a persecution of the " saints," that is, the believers in Christ on earth and is successful (cf. 12 : 17). Like the two witnesses, they too are conquered in this combat by an extreme show of violence. God permits that those who stand by him and his Messiah must pay the highest price of their loyalty, he expects of them the testimony of blood by surrendering their earthly life. Yet the Church and all who declare themselves for her do not live under the anxiety of only a " short time " (12 : 12) which gives all the victories of Satan the stamp of transitoriness; the Christian martyrs know that their names are indelibly inscribed in the " book of life " (cf. 3 : 5); with the Church of Christ they possess the breath of eternity (Mt. 16 : 18).

[7b]*And authority was given it over every tribe and people and tongue and nation, [8]and all who dwell on earth will worship it, everyone whose name has not been written before the foundation of the world in the book of life of the Lamb that was slain.*

By virtue of the employment of demonic power, the beast will succeed in the achievement of that masterpiece, which in the history of mankind has always been desired, and which as such has a positive value, the political unification of the nations on earth linked together by a world-wide system of order. But behind this type of world unification the writer of Revelation sees " the power of darkness " (Lk. 22 : 53); the power potential which the dragon bestows on the beast makes this possible and it pursues with it a very special purpose. With the help of such a universal position of power, the beast has now the opportunity of everywhere demanding divine honors for himself and his patron. Those who " dwell on earth "—a standing expression of Revelation (cf. 6 : 10) which is here defined in contrast with the elect ("everyone whose name has not been written . . . before the foundation of the world ")—the " people of the world " readily adapt themselves to this demand, for to them what is of this world is all that is. But the " saints " do not bend the knee, they remain faithful to their eternal election even under such extreme pressure, they refuse to acknowledge the beast and be subject to it as they are convinced that when their Lord returns at the end of time they will share with him his true sovereignty for all eternity.

9If anyone has an ear, let him hear: 10If anyone is to be taken captive, to captivity he goes; if anyone slays with the sword, with the sword must he be slain. Here is a call for the endurance and the faith of the saints.

Here clear fronts are drawn which exclude every possibility of compromise; those who wish to remain faithful to God and Christ are ostracized by the rest of society. This consequence is drawn in conclusion from what has been revealed; it occurs in the form of an instruction, like the slogans of victory at the end of the seven epistles, which underlines that special attention is required (cf. 2:7 and par).

This instruction is evidently formulated with reference to the two texts in Jeremiah (Jer. 15:2; 43:11) and as to content it says the same here as there: the fate of the conquered is captivity or death; one must therefore be prepared for it.

Under the rule of the antichrist, which will be extensively and intensively all-embracing, the possibility will hardly exist any longer of avoiding the final decision by flight into obscurity. By virtue of the prophetic forecast which Christ has given his Church on her path through history, she is always a " Church without illusions "; she is aware that her lot on earth is like that of her Lord and Master and confronts her fate outwardly without rebellion but with an inner resistance of patient faith. With this insight in mind and with a hope which looks beyond the passing present time to what is coming and will remain the Christian faces even martyrdom, taking it on himself in imitation of " Jesus Christ, the faithful witness " (1 : 4).

The Second Beast, the "Prophet" of the Antichrist (13 : 11–18)

11Then I saw another beast which rose out of the earth; it had two horns like a Lamb and it spoke like a dragon.

Into the vision of the first beast there is inserted a further complementary vision of a second beast. It appears, judging by externals to begin with, quite harmless, namely, in the form of a peaceful, innocent Lamb. Its horns, of course, point to the fact that, in spite of everything, it has something to do with power; only two in number, yet added to those of the first beast, whose functionary it appears to be, the complete number twelve results. With the appearance of the second beast the power of the first is therefore completed. Diadems, the signs of sovereignty, are lacking, for this beast stands wholly at the service of the first; it is appointed to re-enforce and spread the authority of the first.

The prophet sees the second beast rising out of the earth—seen from Patmos, this would indicate Asia Minor in whose centers of culture the evil spirit of the times, including its religious expression (emperor cult), came to light especially concentrated.

That this harmless appearance is only a clever camouflage becomes evident when the beast speaks; it speaks the language of the dragon and thus betrays whose spiritual child it is, to whom it belongs. It is the " theologian of the antichrist " (E. Peterson) and later it is called the " false prophet " (16 : 13; 19 : 20; 20 : 10);

moreover, it appears in a garb pronounced as typical of the lying prophets by the Lord himself (Mt. 7 : 15).

The second beast introduces the first to the world, publicizes its nature and discloses its power. Surely the analogy which exists between the relationships of the two beasts and that of Jesus Christ and the Holy Spirit is not accidental. The counter-image of the true God is now complete with the second beast; the dragon constitutes together with the beasts a " Satanic trinity " (Jung-Stilling).

[12]It exercises all the authority of the first beast in its presence, and makes the earth and its inhabitants worship the first beast, whose mortal wound was healed.

The engagement of the second beast is for the sake of the first beast's seizure of unlimited power; for this purpose it is appointed and equipped by the latter; it must make people acknowledge the first beast as what it pretends to be, namely, God himself. This is the aim of all its propaganda in word and deed; it does not make propaganda for a philosophical ideology, it works for a religious faith. What is at stake is to give a religious aura to the world power of the antichrist and to make people render him cultic veneration. The figure of the " false prophet " therefore takes on priestly features too.

[13]It works great signs, even making fire come down from heaven to earth in the sight of men; [14]and by the signs it is allowed to work in the presence of the beast, it deceives those who dwell on earth, bidding them to make an image for the beast which was wounded by the sword and yet lived; [15]and it was allowed to give breath to the image of the beast so that the image of the beast should even speak, and to cause those who would not worship the image of the beast to be slain. [16]Also it causes all,

*both small and great, both rich and poor, both free and slave,
to be marked on the right hand or the forehead, [17]so that no one
can buy or sell unless he has the mark, that is, the name of the
beast or the number of its name.*

Here we learn the means and measures which the publicity
expert of the antichrist uses to achieve his aim.

Whereas the true Messiah expressly refuses to have his divine
mission attested by miraculous signs (Mt. 6: 1–4 par.), the false
prophet—as is foretold of him in other apocalyptic texts of the
New Testament (Mt. 24: 24 par.; cf. also 2 Thess. 2: 9f.)—
performs great miracles for show which have the desired effect
on the masses; so he even achieves that miracle of Elijah with
which the latter authenticated himself as a prophet of the true
God (3 Kings 18: 38). They need not be the same type of supernatural deeds to make people marvel at, and admire those who
are seeking such; one can well imagine that nowadays " miracles "
of science and technology, quite extraordinary achievements for
the good of human society (social " miracles "), make a similar
impression and fulfill the same purpose. After faith in the antichrist has been awakened, " those who dwell on earth " are
persuaded by his captivating eloquence to let him have his corresponding cult. The state authority raised to divinity by a conscious
manipulation of opinion becomes an idol which must be offered
incense. In the Roman emperor cult, divine honors were shown
the head of state in this way before an image of the emperor
since the holy power of Rome was symbolically expressed in
him and was conceived as permeating the entire ecumenicity;
similarly the image of the seemingly immortal beast keeps its
earthly sovereignty awake in the minds of all and thus keeps
them in bondage.

In this way like a living creature the image creates conviction
and credence, captures the understanding and the heart of people

for him who is represented by it; it controls the mode of thought and power of judgment, it stimulates philosophers and inspires poets. Thus a fundamental attitude is developed in society which is determined and satiated by the spirit of the beast; in the end the general public at large identifies itself with it; for him who is unwilling there is no longer any room in the world community; he pronounces a death sentence on himself. The political symbol raised to a cultic object first makes possible the clear distinction between friend and foe and at the same time delivers the pretext, based on religious grounds, of making every opponent innocuous.

In order to translate into deed the totalitarian claims of the antichrist and to carry through a unitarian acknowledgment of him without exception, the second beast devises a final measure to force all to declare themselves. Everyone who acknowledges the first beast as his god and lord must let this be made visible by an outward mark put on parts of the body which cannot be overlooked or hid, namely, on the right hand or the forehead. In those days animals and slaves were branded as property of their owners; the bearer of this mark of the beast declares himself as belonging to the beast for better or for worse. Indeed, one's life depends on whether one wears it or not; for the precondition of naked existence is withdrawn by economic boycott from those who refuse, they must die of hunger.

Also this last disposition contrived as a very sure coercive measure is again only mimicry in the manner of its execution; it is said of the elect that they bear the seal of their God on their foreheads (7:2f.; 14:1; 22:4), which is a symbol for the fact that by Baptism they were invisibly sealed as children of God.

[18]*This calls for wisdom: let him who has understanding reckon the number of the beast, for it is a human number, its number is six hundred and sixty-six.*

On the devil's monument is engraved the name of the beast, sometimes also concealed in a number. The insight of faith will know how to decipher it when and wherever the beast appears in the shape of a historical man. For the antichrist will always appear as a human being; so much at least is made clear in the otherwise obscure numerical puzzle with the observation that it is " a human number." Names could also have been written as numbers because in antiquity numerals as such were not in use, but the letters of the alphabet were also used as numerical cyphers. To decipher such a secret code was difficult because every number could be broken down into as many terms of a sum as one likes and hence makes possible an equally variegated multiplicity of letter combinations; without the additional information of a key to the division, the discovery of the name was practically impossible.

The first addressees must have been given a clue to recognize who was meant; in any case only a generation later it was impossible to do anything with the number and Irenaeus of Lyon considers therefore all guess work as useless. Instead he tries to find a general eschatological symbolism behind the numbers: 6 is half of the celestial number of perfection 12 (cf. 12:14: half of the number 7 as the number of evil) and at the same time the holy number 7 reduced by 1; written down three times and taking thereby into consideration the symbolism of 3 as a full measure, the number 666 could in Irenaeus' opinion express the nature of the antichrist as the summit of godlessness and of evil of all times. In any case, and Irenaeus also alludes to this, the Christian believers can rest assured that the necessary wisdom will always be supernaturally bestowed on them to recognize the antichrist.

The Lamb and His Followers:
The Preservation of the Church (14:1–5)

In the summarized preview of the climax of the war at the end
of history (11:1–13) an image promising protection and preservation was in front. In the temple an area is staked out which
cannot be taken by the onslaught of the infernal forces (11:7).
This image is once more taken up at the conclusion of the frightful disclosure concerning the antichrist and is further delineated
in a new vision. It gives an answer to the anxious question which
had to arise after the portrayal of the war of annihilation pursued by the Satanic forces with comprehensive possibilities and
infernal hatred (13:1–8): In such circumstances will anything
at all of God's Church be left on earth? This question is
answered in a glowing image, which arouses hope and gives
assurance by representing the elect as safe and sound under the
protection of the Lamb who is in their midst.

*¹Then I looked and lo, on Mount Zion stood the Lamb, and
with him a hundred and forty-four thousand who had his name
and his Father's name written on their foreheads.*

The showplace of the vision is on the earth; it is the mountain
of Zion, the temple mount in Jerusalem (cf. 11:1), which the
prophets had foretold as the place of refuge for the salvation
community of the final time (Jn. 3:5; 4:17); later apocalyptic
writings saw in it the place where the Messiah will appear to
rescue those loyal to him and to sit in judgment on his enemies
(4 Ezra 13:35–40; 5 Ezra 2:42–47); on Zion God will, according to prophetic expectation, finally complete his kingdom
through the Messiah (Is. 24:23; Ps. 2:6; 110 [109]:2f.).

The Lamb is depicted as a victor (cf. 5:5) surrounded by the elect who are gathered about in full number (cf. 7:4). As a sign of their belonging to the Lamb they bear his name together with the name of God written on their foreheads; in the same way the followers of the beast had by a corresponding mark declared themselves bondsmen and property of the antichrist (13:16).

²*And I heard a voice from heaven like the sound of many waters and like the sound of loud thunder; the voice I heard was like the sound of harpers playing on their harps,* ³*and they sing a new song before the throne and before the four living creatures and before the elders. No one could learn the song except the hundred and forty-four thousand who had been redeemed from the earth.*

Although this vision on the earth is seen in the framework of what is transitory, the scene is nevertheless completed bathed in the transfiguring light which falls on it in anticipation of the future consummation; a piece of creation history and human history appears here which in the midst of transitoriness already is essentially in harmony with its final structure, as a voice from heaven expressly indicates. The rumble of powerful thunder has already in earlier images (cf. 4:5; 8:5; 11:19) indicated the awesome majesty of God and the majesty of his celestial world; the word of authority of the transfigured Son of Man, who appears here in the image of the Lamb, had also previously been compared with the sound of many waters (1:15). Sheltered by the omnipotence of God and protected by the love of a saviour who died for them, the followers of the Lamb give the impression of superior composure and imperturbable security.

Through the Lamb in their midst the elect are even on earth linked with the blessed multitude in heaven whose song they hear and can already make their own. It is a " new song," therefore, it sings of a new salvific happening (cf. 5:9); the context admits an insight into its content, it is the song of victory of the final victory of the Lamb and of the forestalled consummation of God's kingdom; to the ears of those who know themselves to be redeemed from the earth ruled by the beast (13:16) it sounds, therefore, like the joy-inspiring song of a vocalist accompanying himself on a harp.

'It is these who have not defiled themselves with woman, for they are chaste; it is these who follow the Lamb wherever he goes; these have been redeemed from mankind as first fruits for God and the Lamb, ⁵and in their mouth no lie was found, for they are spotless.

The portrayal concludes with a characterization of the elect; indirectly it presents a yardstick with which everyone can discern whether he can class himself with them; a plain specification but one which meets all the essentials of what and how Christians are.

They must stand staunchly on the side of Christ; the first thing which is said of them in this symbolic explanation is that they are celibate; in this detail there are echoes of the words of Christ and the apostle Paul who recommends that those who wish to be at the disposal of the Lord and his affairs should remain unmarried (Mt. 19:12; 1 Cor. 7:32–34; 2 Cor. 11:2). Certainly the contrary ideas which arise in the following (14:8) have also a part to play in this; bondage to the beast is expressed there as wooing Babylon which is the symbol for the capital city of the anti-Christian kingdom (cf. 17:2; 18:3. 9; 19:2). Adultery and fornication are frequent images in the prophets of Israel for apostasy and worship of idols (e.g., Hos. 2:14–21; Jer. 2:2–6). The symbolic interpretation of virginity merits priority because in the vision no special group is referred to, rather the Church as a whole appears on the scene. Later too she will be introduced in her entirety in a sense-related image as the bride of the Lamb (19:7; 21:2. 9; 22:17).

The freedom of perfect love binds the elect to their Lord; they stand by him in unconditional obedience and follow him wheresoever he leads. They are ready and shrink back from nothing; even if he leads them on the path he trod himself as man via persecution and death to glorification, they will not refuse the testimony of blood.

It was prescribed in the law for the people of Israel that they offer the first ripe fruits of every harvest to God as a sign that everything belongs to him (Lev. 23:9-14). In God's eyes this elite of mankind appears as that gift of first fruits; chosen from the whole, they already belong to God and the Lamb as entirely his own (cf. 1 Pet. 2:9f.). Considered in the context, the gift of first fruits means still more. With them a start is made in bringing the entire world into God's kingdom; hence they stand before the world as a sign of hope and promise of a redeemed future for the entire creation of God; for in them the absolute future which God has disclosed in Christ is already made present.

As indicative of the fellowship of the Lamb a fourth characteristic is named: absolute truthfulness. He who belongs to God whose nature is truth and dependability can have nothing in common with the " father of lies " (Jn. 8:44), that is to say, with Satan whose nature is based on the lie. Purity in thought and sentiment, truthfulness in word, dependability in trade and traffic, simplicity of nature in which word and deed do not part, in short: the upright personality on whom one can depend (5:37; Jas. 5:12), who can stand in the light of God who is truth (Ps. 43 [42] :3).

Summarizing, the text reads that they are entirely spotless. If sacrificial animals of the old Covenant had to be without spot (Ex. 12:5; Lev. 23:12f.) then this requirement applies all the more to the " first fruits " of the consummated Covenant who make up the followers of the " Lamb without blemish and spot " (1 Pet. 1 : 19).

The inner reality of the " community of saints," of the Church of Christ, is fully described in the few lines of this image. The faithful already stand in the sanctuary, in God's kingdom, lovingly united to the Lord in their midst, who is their shepherd and saviour. In the midst of the world and active in and for the world they are not bondsmen of the " god of this world " (2 Cor. 4 : 4), as " redeemed from the earth " they follow " the Lamb wherever he goes."

PREPARATION FOR THE FINAL JUDGMENT
(14:6—19:10)

The two camps have been described, the fronts staked out; the "little flock" (Lk. 12:32) following the Lamb has been promised protection; the final combat can now start.

Preview of the Final Judgment (14:6–20)

The Announcement of the Judgment (14: 6–13)

⁶Then I saw another angel flying in midheaven, with an eternal gospel to proclaim to those who dwell on earth, to every nation and tribe and tongue and people; ⁷and he said with a loud voice, Fear God and give him glory, for the hour of his judgment has come; and worship him who made heaven and earth, the sea and the fountains of water.

Four messages are sent from heaven in this section, the first and last have salvation as subject, the second and third the judgment; the first three are imparted by the angels, the last by the voice of someone invisible. The first angel flies high at the zenith where the eagle flew who called down the threefold woe audible to the whole earth (8:13); like the message of the eagle that of the angel concerns also all "those who dwell on earth," that is, according to apocalyptic usage: people who do not want to know about God. The message of the angel is in contrast with that of the eagle a promise of salvation; it is based on God's eternal counsel, its subject is eternal salvation. Through

the angel, God offers it to everyone who before the end decides
to be converted to him; this is his last invitation before it is too
late.

The invitation is reminiscent of the angelic hymn which in
the gospel interprets the significance of the birth of Jesus
(Lk. 2:14); in substance it is like the sermon of the Baptist
(Mt. 3:1) which Jesus again took up in his preaching (Mt. 4:17).
To give God the glory that is due to him is the way to avoid
the judgment and to arrive at eternal salvation. Fear of God
and worship of him are the basic requirements of Old Testament piety from which Christian propagation has retracted
nothing.

To substantiate his call the angel addresses himself to an
understanding of history which is already found in the Old
Testament revelation and from there has become typical of the
Christian view of the world. In contrast with the Greek heathen
concept of the world and history which conceives the course of
history as a continuous chain of cycles closed within themselves
of becoming and passing away, the Biblical idea represents it as
linear, as a movement towards a final point. This conviction,
which provides the entire process with a goal, is connected with
the other that this course has been set in motion by God's act
of creation; in such a beginning the goal is also fixed; in such
a goal is enclosed the entire meaning of the process of history;
hence the true meaning of world history can only be grasped
from its end. The end, moreover, which at the same time is a
consummation, is not automatically reached by progressive
development but is promoted by new actions and finally by the
intervention of God himself.

The final goal of world, and especially of human history, is
seen by revelation to reside concretely in that " God is everything to everyone," that is, the realization of the consummated
kingdom of God. This idea only becomes specifically Christian

when the further conviction is added that with the person and work of Jesus Christ the future kingdom of God, that is, the final goal, has already made an appearance here and now although still only in a temporal manner. What implications this fact has in history are clarified in the apocalyptic images which now follow (14:8—19:10); thus they give an answer to the question: What actually happens in history?

⁸Another angel, a second, followed, saying, Fallen, fallen is Babylon the great, she made all nations drink the wine of her impure passion.

The call of the second angel proclaims a judgment already executed. A prophetic prediction in the true sense, it is, however, given in the past tense to indicate the absolute certainty of its happening; its content moreover is stylistically stressed as especially important by a solemn repetition.

The judgment refers to Babylon; Old Testament prophecy already uses this great city symbolically—the dark counterpart of Jerusalem, the city of God—as the place of godlessness. The call of the angel, therefore, takes pattern from the wording of that type of prophetic text (Is. 21:9; Jer. 51:7; Dan. 4:27). With an equally traditional image (cf. Jer. 51:7) her guilt is specified; it consisted of the seduction of the whole world to the worship of idols which had its beginning in her; the image of the " wine of wrath " already implies that such apostasy bears its judgment within it.

The name Babylon survived the historical city as a symbol and functioned in the Jewish apocalypse as a pseudonym for Rome, as for instance in the First Letter of St. Peter (1 Pet. 5:13). It has, to begin with, the same symbolic meaning in John's Revelation but in addition it reaches beyond this historical limitation, as will be seen later (17:1—18:24). Babylon, the capital city of the beast's kingdom (17:1ff.), stands in history, not only of that time but for all time, fundamentally in opposition to Mount Zion, the Lamb's fortress (14:1–5).

⁹And another angel, a third, followed them, saying with a loud voice, If anyone worships the beast and its image, and receives a mark on his forehead or on his hand, ¹⁰he also shall drink the wine of God's wrath, poured unmixed into the cup of his anger, and shall be tormented with fire and brimstone in the presence of the holy angels and in the presence of the lamb. ¹¹And the smoke of their torment goes up for ever and ever; and they have no rest, day or night, these worshippers of the beast and its image, and whoever receives the mark of his name.

The third angel turns to all worshippers of the beast with a warning (cf. 13:12) whether they be followers out of conviction or fellow travelers out of cowardice. They have not only betrayed God and his Christ but themselves too as God's image and likeness (Gen. 1:26) in addition, inasmuch as they are Christians, the likeness of his Son which was stamped on them like a seal at Baptism. For such sacrilege the wine of God's wrath will be given them " unmixed," not thinned out with water; without grace and mercy the judgment will be pronounced on them.

The description of their punishment is reminiscent of the destruction of Sodom and Gomorrah (Gen. 19:24); like the inhabitants of these cities they will be tormented in infernal fires (19:20; 20:10. 15; cf. Is. 34:9f.). The peculiar addendum : " in the presence of the holy angels and in the presence of the Lamb " probably means that the damned could never forget that they were redeemed and in what manner and how persistently God tried their life long to save them; the angels of God remind them of this as it is said of them in the Letter to the Hebrews they are " sent forth to serve, for the sake of those who are to

obtain salvation " (Heb. 1:4). In the knowledge that they alone
are to blame for their fate, their hate turns against themselves.
What is hardest in their punishment is that it lasts forever; there
is no revision of a sentence which specifies a never ending
execution. In the gospel of redemption we also hear the message
of hell because this gospel is aware of human freedom.

*12Here is a call for the endurance of the saints, those who keep
the commandments of God and the faith of Jesus. 13And I heard
a voice from heaven saying, Write this : Blessed are the dead
who die in the Lord henceforth. Blessed indeed, says the Spirit,
that they may rest from their labors, for their deeds follow them!*

In the face of the frightful end of the damned, the Seer repeats
his call for endurance with which he also concluded the description of the rule of force of the first beast (13:10); an indication
that faith must measure up to a test in which human existence
as such is at stake.

A voice from heaven confirms the exhortation of the pastor
concerned about the Christian's loyalty to the faith in a beatitude
addressed to those who endure persecution to the point of a
violent death of witness. The voice addresses the request to John
to make special mention in his writings of the attestation of his
call which is evidently given by God himself. A second infallible
witness to the truth vouches for it, namely, the same prophetic
spirit who also dictated the victor-text in the seven letters (cf.
2:7). According to the precept of the law (Deut. 17:6; 19:15;
Jn. 8:17), two witnesses who are in agreement validly guarantee
the truth; the express statement of the legally valid attestation
once more underlines how seriously one should take the exhortation. The Spirit testifies in the form of a promise like in the
victor-texts. Death is not the end but a transition from the temporal to what is final. The final state of the damned was de-

scribed as a restless torment (14:11); in contrast, the eternal destiny of those who through effort and final commitment have become blessed appears here as an inner peace and a secured freedom. Their labors, the achievements of their lives wrought in courageous faith, have followed them to the judgment throne of God and have been decisive in determining their eternal bliss.

Preliminary Glimpse of the Execution of Judgment (14:14–20)

In a new vision John is already permitted to look at the process of judgment in general outline which will later be shown him in detail (19:11—20-15). The metaphorical motif of the harvest used in the Old as well as the New Testament to describe the judgment provides here too the framework for the delineation. In a judgment text of the prophet Joel (Joel 4:13) we already find the division into the twofold harvest of corn and wine. On this ground-plan two images of harvest are created here which differing from the prophetic text also refer to two different judgment procedures: the first portrays in the image of the corn harvest the bringing home of the elect (14:14–16), the second image of the wine harvest and the wine press portrays the judgment on the damned (14:17–20).

¹⁴Then I looked, and lo, a white cloud, and seated on the cloud one like a son of man, with a golden crown on his head, and a sharp sickle in his hand.

To begin with the chief character in this judicial trial appears; he is given a name and in addition he is introduced with a title of majesty. The center and pivot of the entire vision (14:6–20) has thereby been staked out; this also indicates the external division of the section: three angels appear before the appearance of the " son of man," three follow.

In the vocation-vision Christ was introduced with the same name as here (1:13) and already in the introduction he was announced as the one who is coming with the clouds of heaven (1:7); the two instances rely on the son of man vision in Daniel (Dan. 7:13) which Jesus himself alluded to when he prophesied his own return to judge the world (Mt. 24:30 par.; 26:64 par.). The Messiah-judge appears crowned with a golden crown, a sign of victory and sovereignty; in his hand he holds a harvest sickle as a symbol of his judicial office.

15And another angel came out of the temple, calling with a loud voice to him who sat upon the cloud, Put in your sickle, and reap, for the hour to reap has come, for the harvest of the earth is fully ripe. 16So he who sat upon the cloud swung his sickle down to earth, and the earth was reaped.

The fourth angel comes out of the temple, that is, from the place of God's presence (7:15; 11:19). He passes on, with words which remain within the metaphor of the harvest, the command of the Father, who alone determines the hour (Mt. 24:36 par.), to the Son of man to begin the judgment. With a sign from him the judgment is set in motion and is at once completed. The image presupposes that the wheat harvest is not brought in by the mandator himself but by reapers; in Jesus' portraits of the judgment—more detailed but with the same metaphor—angels are mentioned as reapers (Mt. 13:39. 41. 49; 24:31 par.). The one enthroned on the white cloud presides and gives command while angels execute the judicial sentence.

17And another angel came out of the temple in heaven, and he too had a sharp sickle. 18Then another angel came out from the altar, the angel who has power over fire, and he called with a loud voice to him who had the sharp sickle, Put in your sickle, and gather the clusters of the vine on earth, for its grapes are ripe. [19]*So the angel swung his sickle on the earth, and gathered the vintage on the earth, and threw it into the great wine press of the wrath of God;* [20]*and the wine press was trodden outside the city, and blood flowed from the wine press, as high as a horse's bridle for one thousand six hundred stadia.*

The image of the wine harvest does not merely underline as a material repetition the meaning of the first, the wheat harvest. The sketch, rather, puts forward a different situation from the first. The judgment refers to a different group of people to those in the first image. The Son of man no longer presides over this judgment, rather an angel receives the command from God through another to give the sign for the harvest and bring it in. Two things are said of the angel who passes on the command: he comes from the altar, that is, from the place at whose foot the souls of the martyrs had asked for vengeance on the persecutors soon (6:9f.); besides this it is said of him that he has power over fire (cf. 7:1). This brings to mind the angel who in an earlier vision, after he had put the " prayers of the saints " on the altar of heaven, took fire from the altar and threw it on the earth after which God's wrathful judgment was manifest in earthly catastrophes (8:3–5). The second image of judgment, which is much more thoroughly filled in, embraces also the delineation of the execution of judgment. All this indicates a special stress in the context of the whole. Finally, the intended meaning strongly colors the image as is indicated by the expressions, " wine press of the wrath of God " and " blood "; hence no doubt can exist that it deals with the judgment on the ungodly. This, moreover, confirms the supposition that in the judgment image of the wheat harvest, which is painted in lighter colors, the bringing home of the elect was being portrayed (cf. Mt. 24:31 par.; 13:30 and 3:12).

The construction of the image has also been influenced by its Old Testament models (besides Joel 4:13, 46 especially Is. 63: 1–6). Also the " grapes " of evil God lets grow to ripeness (cf. Mt. 13:30) before they are pressed " outside the city." The prophet Joel places the judgment on the heathen before the walls of Jerusalem in the valley of Jahoshaphat (Joel 4:2. 12); in Joel too we find the image of the overflowing vat (Joel 4:13); it is meant to convey the impression of extensive destruction. Above all the stream of blood, given in measurements of depth and length—the image comes from Jewish apocalyptic—illustrates the measure and terrifying nature of this judgment; the symbolic detail of the number of stadia—1 stadium = 192 m— consisting of the world number four multiplied by itself and then by a hundred, serves the same purpose; together with the symbol of world-wideness contained in it, it indicates that no ungodly human being will escape the judgment.

God's judgment is as great as God himself. Its execution has two sides, a bright side: the election, and a dark side, the rejection. The decision of the court of justice depends on the prior decision of man for or against him who was consciously placed into the center of this vision; salvation or damnation is dependent on one's attitude to Christ who is the centre of the universe and its history.

The Bowl-Visions (15:1 —16:21)

After the announcement (14:6–12) and preview (14:14–20) of the judgment what has been cursively considered in outline, call to repentance, Babylon's downfall, judgment on the ungodly, is now filled in with individual images. The last call to repentance (14:6f.) corresponds to the unfolding of that call to do penance which is given in the form of a final warning action of God (the bowl-plagues). One can infer that also the last in this series of seven of God's means of chastisement (seal and trumpet plagues)—although they are all also expressions of God's wrath on human perversion and wickedness—have just as the preceding ones not punishment but repentance for final purpose; according to God's design they are finally intended as visitation for salvation. In the treatment of the catastrophic events this is expressly alluded to in three statements to the effect that this purpose had not been achieved (16:9. 11. 21).

¹Then I saw another portent in heaven, great and wonderful, seven angels with seven plagues, which are the last, for with them the wrath of God is ended.

The first verse after the manner of a headline declares the content of the whole section 15:1—16:21. Besides this, the explanation is added that the bowl-plagues are the final chastisement of God before the judgment of the world and its end. To this is connected the fact that no limitation as to extent and space is decreed for them as was for the seal and trumpet plagues; they strike the entire universe and on earth the catastrophes are especially directed against the kingdom of the beast. By the destruction, God already clears away impediments in the way of his final assumption of sovereignty. God leads a counterattack against the attempt of the world to barricade itself against the absolute future of God. A world which in its self-sufficiency and independence shuts itself off from God will have its barricades demolished and its anti-Christian buildup effectively impeded and destroyed.

As already stated, these hard measures pursue in the case of human beings primarily the aim of giving them a shock to make them come to their senses. But since mankind experiences them as severe chastisements, they also bear the stamp of punishment and are revealed to men as God's wrathful judgment. Inasmuch as the wrath of God temporarily reveals itself in the course of world history and the interventions of God indicate and promote the actual " day of wrath when God's righteous judgment will be revealed " (Rom. 2:5), world history can be designated as a provisional, anticipated judgment of the world.

John sees in this vision a significant process (" portent ") which takes place in heaven (cf. 12:1. 3); because what he sees transcends the frame and possibility of nature he calls it " great and wonderful " : seven angels stand ready at the vault of heaven to set in motion the last plagues.

Prelude in Heaven (15: 2–8)

Just as an image of heaven was inserted as interlude before the two other series of seven plagues so here too before the last series of plagues; and just as above it is done with the same purpose of encouragement and consolation in mind.

²And I saw what appeared to be a sea of glass mingled with fire, and those who had conquered the beast and its image and the number of its name, standing beside the sea of glass with harps of God in their hands. ³And they sing the song of Moses, the servant of God, and the song of the Lamb, saying, Great and wonderful are thy deeds, O Lord God the Almighty! Just and true are thy ways, O King of the ages! ⁴Who shall not fear and glorify thy name, O Lord? For thou alone art holy. All nations shall come and worship thee, for thy judgments have been revealed.

Before John sees the seven angels at work he obtains revelation of a celestial event which unfolds in two scenes. He first sees the blessed company of those who prevailed in the combat against the beast and have died " in the Lord " (14:13) and are now in glory with God.

Correspondingly, the scene of the vision is God's throne-room; the floor, the vault of heaven, is described with the same comparison as earlier on (cf. 4:6), but here there is the addendum: the crystal clear gleaming surface sparkles with a fiery-red glow; just as the evening glow announced the end of a day, so it proclaims before the Lord of time and eternity (cf. 4:8: " who is and was and is to come ") the end of the world and the imminent judgment.

The transfigured company of heroes on the fiery, glowing floor sings its hymn of victory before him who has saved them. The three part enumeration (" the beast and its image and the number of its name ") names the foe over which they triumphed; at the same time, it once more recalls forcibly to their minds their, as to external circumstances, quite hopeless situation in the past. Impotent themselves they were rescued by the omnipotence of the Most High as the people of God of the old Covenant were before them, when the might of Pharaoh threatened to annihilate them at the Sea of Reeds. Therefore, they sing their hymn of victory as a hymn of gratitude to him who sits on the throne; he has saved them. In its wording the hymn relies throughout on Old Testament songs of praise and celebrates with these venerable texts of the people of the first Covenant the majesty and holiness of the creator of the world as well as the righteousness and sovereignty of the director of history.

The double name (" song of Moses," " song of the Lamb ") expressly links that act of rescue in the old Covenant with that which is celebrated here. Above all the special manner in which God performed the rescue is given prominence in both instances. In the past it occurred through Moses sent by him to his people as their leader and now through his Son sent into the world for that purpose, whose vicarious sacrificial death accomplished the redemption ("Lamb"). As a type, the first act of rescue throws its light on the second final rescue. Just as Moses intoned the song of thanksgiving after the crossing of the Sea of Reeds in the midst of, and in the name of those saved (Ex. 15:1–18) so does the Lamb now in the midst of the transfigured company of combatants who have achieved victory through it (cf. 14:1–5).

In this scene, for the second time, the victory of Christ which is still to come to decide everything is anticipated as already present (cf. 14:1–5); in this way believers in Christ are strengthened with prophetic certainty in the hope of a quite sure final salvation, before they, together with unbelievers, are led into the difficult times of the now dawning day of God's final judgment.

⁵After this I looked, and the temple of the tent of witness was opened, ⁶and out of the temple came the seven angels with the seven plagues, robed in pure linen, and their breasts girded with golden girdles. ⁷And one of the living creatures gave the seven angels seven golden bowls full of the wrath of God who lives for ever and ever;

The second scene gives an account of the solemn framework in which the equipment of the seven angels takes place. The portal of the celestial temple (cf. 11:19) opens and John sees the original tent whereby Moses in the past constructed the tent of the Covenant at God's request (Ex. 25:9. 40; Heb. 8:5) because in it he desired to give witness of his presence to his people in their trek through the wilderness by revelations and deeds of power.

Out of this he saw emerging seven angels in priestly garments (cf. 1:13); they come from a priestly service before the Most High to continue with it in the fulfillment of their task in regard to the earth (cf. 8:2–5) for which they bring seven plagues with them. They come therefore from God and do their service before the " king of nations " who is holy in his essence and just in his ways (cf. 15 : 3f.).

One of the four living creatures, who stand in a special relation to the creation (cf. 4 : 7), equip them for their task (cf. 6 : 1–8); seven celestial bowls (" golden ") which contain the " wrath of God " are given them. When poured out of the bowls, it will strike mankind judging and punishing.

[8]*and the temple was filled with smoke from the glory of God and from his power, and no one could enter the temple until the seven plagues of the seven angels were ended.*

As an outward sign of the presence of the glory and power of the Most High the Seer sees the temple filling with smoke; this makes it impossible for any human being to enter. While the bowl-plagues take their course God is unapproachable; no prayer or meditation can turn aside his chastisement.

The Execution of the Bowl-Plagues: the Third Woe (16 : 1–21)

The seventh trumpet call, with which the last woe was to have begun (11 : 14) and the " mystery of God " was to have been " fulfilled " (cf. 10 : 6f.), had already been given (11 : 15); but nothing was said of the happenings which were set in motion thereby. Immediately linked to this was a provisional glimpse of the last goal of creation, as if already reached (11 : 19), where in a hymn the Almighty is thanked for the consummated salvation in the completed kingdom of God. In conclusion, the account once more returned to the reality of the provisional world while the outstanding catastrophes, which the last trumpet call had announced, were at least symbolically alluded to (11 : 19b). The series of images now beginning here take up from there; they fill in the missing account of the third woe; the individual delineations unfold the course of the history of the end up to the anticipated final goal (11 : 15–19a).

The author of Revelation remains true to himself in the form of presentation; just as the new group of seven, the trumpet plagues emerged from the breaking of the seventh seal, so the third group of seven, the bowl visions arise from the seventh trumpet vision.

The bowl visions run quite parallel to the trumpet visions in sequence and content, just as both also rely very closely on the same Biblical text, the account of the Egyptian plagues (cf. 8 : 7–12); but with regard to extent and severity, the last plagues are aggravated to the highest degree in view of the approaching end of the world.

¹Then I heard a loud voice from the temple telling the seven angels, Go and pour on the earth the seven bowls of the wrath of God.

God himself gives the order (" a loud voice from the temple ") to pour out the bowls; the word of the creator himself initiates the final process whereby his creation is transformed from its provisional into its consummated form.

²So the first angel went and poured his bowl on the earth, and foul and evil sores came upon the men who bore the mark of the beast and worshipped its image. ³The second angel poured his bowl into the sea, and it became like the blood of a dead man, and every living thing died that was in the sea. ⁴The third angel poured his bowl into the rivers and the fountains of water, and they became blood.

In line with the trumpet plagues, the first four bowl plagues strike the earth, the sea, fresh water and the sun. They all accomplish an all-embracing destruction.

Of the first plague, we read, that it strikes only those whose inner foulness now appears outwardly in the form of foul sores. The second changes all sea water into blood, indeed, into the putrefying blood of a corpse which has a deadly effect on all life in the sea. The third spoils the fresh water changing it into blood; he who does not want to perish from thirst must drink it.

5And I heard the angel of water say, Just art thou in these thy judgments, thou art and wast, O Holy One. 6For men have shed the blood of saints and prophets, and thou hast given them blood to drink. It is their due! 7And I heard the altar cry, Yea, Lord God the Almighty, true and just are thy judgments!

Two prayers in the form of a responsorium acknowledge the justice of these judgments of God. Even the angel who was put in charge of the waters (cf. 7:1) must testify that the pollution of his element is just. As already in 11:17, the third part (" who is to come ") of God's appellation is missing here; for now he is coming. The followers of the beast have made war on the " saints " (cf. 13:7) and on the " prophets " (cf. 11:7) and have killed them; if they now must drink blood themselves it is a just punishment for murderers. This drastic mode of expression is, of course, in line with the apocalyptic form of presentation, meant only as a metaphor and in substance it says no more than that in God's court of justice the yardstick of absolute justice is what counts. From the altar, at whose foot the souls of God's blood witnesses had prayed for justice (cf. 6:9f.), the affirmation of the angel's word comes like an echo.

8The fourth angel poured his bowl on the sun, and it was allowed to scorch men with fire; 9men were scorched by the fierce heat,

*and they cursed the name of God who had power over these
plagues, and they did not repent and give him glory.*

The fourth bowl is poured on the sun; its content has the effect
of oil thrown on a fire, not reducing the sun's brightness like in
the corresponding trumpet plague, but increasing its heat to a
blaze which scorches everything.

In this final time God's chastisements no longer urge men,
as formerly (cf. 11:13), to repent and be converted; those who
are impervious in their wickedness, who well know who sends
them these chastisements and why he sends them, utter only
blasphemies and curses.

[10]*The fifth angel poured his bowl on the throne of the beast, and
its kingdom was in darkness; men gnawed their tongues in
anguish* [11]*and cursed the God of heaven for their pain and sores,
and did not repent of their deeds.*

The fifth angel pours his bowl on the throne of the beast; the
world power which is at Satan's command experiences for the
first time that limits are imposed on its power despite the
shrewdest calculations, consequential planning and comprehensive regulations. That splendor, which was displayed as a matter
of course, suffers an eclipse; men suddenly feel insecure when
that on which they set their entire faith and based all their hope
becomes obscure; unbearable physical pain is added as torment.
These remarks, however, are too terse for any more definite
statement on the topic. Probably, details from the corresponding
trumpet plague, which was filled in with greater detail, could be
used to understand this one. The use of more severe means of
chastisement does not accomplish a conversion, it only fans their
rebellion against God to a bitter anger. That God, who was

deposed and declared " dead," is there again and responsible
for everything!

[12]*The sixth angel poured his bowl on the great river Euphrates,
and its water was dried up, to prepare the way for the kings of
the east.* [13]*And I saw, issuing from the mouth of the dragon and
from the mouth of the beast and from the mouth of the false
prophet, three foul spirits like frogs;* [14]*for they are demonic spirits
performing signs, who go abroad to the kings of the whole
world, to assemble them for battle on the great day of God the
Almighty.* [15]*(Lo, I am coming like a thief! Blessed is he who is
awake, keeping his garments that he may not go naked and be
seen exposed!)* [16]*And they assembled at the place which is called
in Hebrew Armageddon.*

The sixth bowl plague is described in greater detail. The preceding one struck the holder of world power; this new one refers to
the associates and instruments of the world power in the service
of Satan.

With the drying up of the river Euphrates (cf. Is. 11:15; Jer.
51:36) the barrier is removed which up till now stood in the
way of a gathering of the entire power-potential of the antichrist.
The powerful of the world, who had put themselves at the
service of the " Satanic trinity " (cf. 13:11), believe that the
favorable moment had arrived to lead a final united attack of
destruction against the Church of God on earth. The Satanic
trinity doubles its propaganda for this purpose; three additional
recruiters and war-mongers are employed, demonic spirits which
issue from them, spirit of their spirit. The new recruit leaders
have the shape of frogs; in the religion of the Persians who dwelt
east of the Euphrates (" the kings of the east ") frogs were considered to be the instrument of Ahriman, the god of darkness;
that would seem to be the reason why the " three foul spirits "
appear here in the form of that amphibian.

Their recruitment drive is successful. The whole world has come as one man and all the power of the world is led into battle against God and those who have remained loyal to him. Armageddon is named as battle field by Revelation, translated it literally means, " mount of Megiddo " (cf. 2 Chr. 35:22). At the Israelite fortress Megiddo at the south east strand of the plain of Esdrelon many historic battles had taken place; this may have been the stimulus to give this symbolic name to the place of the decisive battle of the end of time.

Until this final battle of history, Armageddon will be contemporary whenever the collected forces of evil attack God and the Church of his Son, just as, on the other hand, Zion is always a reality wherever the Church flocks in unity and faith around its shepherd, Christ (cf. 14:1-5).

The apparent detail of place, Armageddon, awakens the still more urgently felt desire for information as to time. This desire is met by the warning of Christ, which receives here an unheralded insertion into the description and which conveys: it will definitely come, it will be unexpected (" like a thief "; cf. 3:3) and sudden, that is, at a time which cannot be predicted or calculated (cf. Mt. 24:36 par.; 1 Thess. 5:2-11). Hence the glorified Lord repeats the exhortation to watchfulness and readiness which he had already addressed to his disciples in his lifetime in similar circumstances (cf. Mt. 24:42 par.).

An alert Christian expectantly takes notice of all the signs of the future of Christ announcing itself in history; he discovers in every passing moment of this time, as it approaches its future goal, the challenge of a decision for the coming Lord. To meet every challenge means to be ready for his coming like someone who stands dressed and equipped, waiting for him who will fetch him. He who lives his life in this manner is called blessed because he has used the passing time in the proper way for his own eternity.

¹⁷The seventh angel poured his bowl into the air, and a great voice came out of the temple, from the throne, saying, It is done! ¹⁸And there were flashes of lightning, loud noises, peals of thunder, and a great earthquake such as had never been since men were on earth, so great was the earthquake. ¹⁹The great city was split into three parts, and the cities of the nations fell, and God remembered great Babylon, to make her drain the cup of the fury of his wrath. ²⁰And every island fled away and no mountains were to be found; ²¹and great hailstones, heavy as a hundred weight, dropped on men from heaven, till men cursed God for the plague of the hail, so fearful was that plague.

The cosmic upheavals reach their climax (cf. 6:12–17), after which the earth is no longer recognizable; a tremendous field of rubble is left. Of the damage which the capital city of the antichrist suffered one is especially mentioned: the earthquake had split it into three parts; the first decisive thrust against the outer unity and, simultaneously, against the inner uniformity of the antitheistic world power has been delivered. Till now it seemed at times as if this center of godlessness and corruption had been forgotten by God. Now it is taken to task; the judgment meted out to it will subsequently be described in greater detail (17:1—19:10).

Just as a hail-storm with stones of a hundred weight would destroy everything on earth, so these last cosmic blows of destruction reduce everything to rubble that nature and culture had produced on earth; this earthly collapse announces the end of the world; time has now for ever expired for those who have rejected all God's gifts of grace and now curse him in their imperviousness.

The Judgment on Babylon (17:1—19:10)

Those measures of God, which were intended as a last jog to the ungodly to change their minds and repent before the imminent final judgment, have now with the bowl-plagues passed over without success; because of the stubborn imperviousness of the beast worshippers, these already bore the stamp of punitive measures; they already initiated the final arrangements to create free space for the definitive and new reconstruction of the world. This cleansing of God's creation from everything that is hostile to God is set forth in what follows; the delineation moves thereby in reverse order from that of the take over process of the world by the forces hostile to God. At first we hear how its central stronghold on earth, the capital city of the antichrist, is annihilated; after that there is an account of the elimination and condemnation of the dragon's auxiliary forces and finally of the final prostration of the dragon himself.

This then has created the presupposition for the final separation of good and evil at the world judgment; with this again the pre-condition is fulfilled for the establishment of God's consummated kingdom.

The Image of the Great Harlot Babylon
and Its Interpretation (17 : 1–18)

¹*Then one of the seven angels who had the seven bowls came and said to me, Come, I will show you the judgment of the great harlot who is seated upon many waters, ²with whom the kings of the earth have committed fornication, and with the wine of whose fornication the dwellers on earth have become drunk.*

The last bowl plague had already started the judgment of Babylon (16:19), which had previously already been announced by an angel (14:8). However, before it is described in a strikingly broad and gripping portrayal (18:1–19:10), the prophet unfolds an image of the residence of the antichrist which is shown to him by one of the bowl angels in a symbolic presentation. The description of the image (17:1–6) is therefore followed by the angel's interpretation (17:7–18), which in spite of its thoroughness holds much that is obscure for us today and leaves some questions unanswered.

The first two verses are once more a headline (as in 15:1) which announces the theme and also posts ahead some significant clues for understanding.

When in Old Testament writings the ungodly, and especially the antitheistic nature of a city is to be pilloried it often happens that it is called a harlot; this is what is intended here with the designation.

The description of Babylon's situation (" upon many waters ") relies on Jer. 51:13; it refers externally to the extensive network of canals of the Euphrates which ran through the city and surrounds. This detail was already meant symbolically in Jeremiah; equally so, it is later on in Revelation (v. 15) interpreted symbolically as indicating her sovereignty over all nations of the world; the close connection of Babylon with the " cities of the nations " was already alluded to in 16:19; the city of Babylon represents the entire sphere over which she rules. From this we infer: Babylon is imagined as possessing political greatness of world-wide influence.

As the power center of the antitheistic world she has infected all the " dwellers on earth " (cf. 3:10) with her antitheistic and immoral spirit (cf. 14:8; 18:3); she keeps this spirit alive through her bondsmen, the " kings of the earth " who employ their power everywhere for this purpose.

³And he carried me away in the Spirit into a wilderness, and I saw a woman sitting on a scarlet beast which was full of blasphemous names and it had seven heads and ten horns.

The details of the heading are now singly explained by a more detailed description of an image seen in a vision with an added interpretation. The vision begins with an ecstatic experience (cf. 4:1f.); from the platform of the wilderness, stretching from Palestine to Mesopotamia, John is shown what he describes in what follows; it was precisely from this wilderness that Isaiah saw the judgment on Babel (Is. 21:1–10).

The capital of the antichrist, in which the antitheistic world empire is, as it were, concentrated, appears in the symbol of a woman. She is consciously drawn in contrast to the other woman in ch. 12, the symbol of the Church of God, and also to a further symbolic figure of a woman which later on expresses the relationship between Christ and his Church, to the " bride of Christ " (21:9ff.). Surrender to the will of God and her Lord Jesus Christ characterizes the Church, surrender to the will of Satan is the essential mark of the counterchurch of the antichrist; hence the latter is shown as a harlot in the image of perverted feminine self-surrender (cf. 14:4).

The woman rides on a beast; riding goddesses were not infrequent in ancient Oriental illustrations. A closer description of the animal immediately identifies it as a beast out of the bottomless pit (13:1–10). The color alone, but above all the blasphemous names with which not only its head (cf. 13:1) but its entire body is smeared, characterizes it as a type related to Satan. The beast carries the harlot on its back; the world empire of the final time and its capital are founded in the spirit and the power of Satan.

⁴The woman was arrayed in purple and scarlet, and bedecked

*with gold and jewels and pearls, holding in her hand a golden
cup full of abominations and the impurities of her fornication; . . .*

Her whole appearance identifies the woman as a tasteless monstrosity; in whose service she is, is indicated by some drastic
addenda.

The twin-colored attire shows the color of sovereignty (purple)
and the color of the beast (v. 3) on which she sits. Spruced up
and overloaded with valuable jewelry, the adornments of the
earth—the woman of 12: 1 reflects the brilliance of heavenly light
—she parades herself in the unlimited possession and enjoyment
of the goods of this world. The excess and obtrusiveness of the
pomp make her already suspect to the sober intelligence: all this
supports the suspicion that we have here an overcompensation
for the poverty and emptiness, the ugliness and insecurity of her
inner being. Finally the content of the cup which the harlot
clutches in her hand confirms the suspicion of a deep-seated
corruption, with which she has intoxicated the whole world. In
final analysis, the content of the cup indicates the same as was
expressed by the symbol of the harlot, namely, godlessness, which
not seldom goes hand in hand with immorality, but which is
not here the immediate consideration.

⁵ *. . . and on her forehead was written a name of mystery :
Babylon the great, mother of harlots and of earth's abominations.*

In those days the harlots of the city of Rome used to wear a
headband on which their name was written. On the headband
of the harlot, John reads the name Babylon, with an additional
mark which exposes her as the very basis and source of all
depravity and hostility to God.

About the name Babylon, the Seer remarks that it is a

" mystery " : he does not, therefore, mean the historical Babylon which even at that time belonged to the past; we are dealing rather with a pseudonym which conceals a city of John's own historical present. Concretely, Rome is meant here (cf. 14 : 8), the capital of the Roman Empire which with its emperor cult bound all its subjects to compulsory idolatry. As almost always in Revelation the symbol reaches beyond the unique historical situation and becomes a criterion valid for all ages. History does not repeat itself. It is precisely the nature of history that it deals with a unique occurrence in unique circumstances. But despite all concrete uniqueness, on another more fundamental level, something similar can occur everytime. There runs parallel with the process of history—so revelation sees it and it is essential to its concept of history—a reality which is present in each transitory manifestation; it harbors within it the real event behind any event. This process in depth is however not immediately discernible, it can only be grasped and represented by way of symbols. Connected with this is Revelation's manner of presentation; it highlights the typical character of world process in any historically unique event which is thereby generalized into allegorical ciphers. One can, therefore, recognize in the Rome of the Emperor Domitian, " the one gruesome, drunken world metropolis of all ages."

[6a]*And I saw the woman, drunk with the blood of the saints and the blood of the martyrs of Jesus.*

A final stroke which is added to the sketch of the great harlot completes the repulsive picture : she is drunk, indeed, intoxicated with the blood of Christians and the messengers of the gospel (" witnesses of Jesus ") which she has had killed.

The false redemptive theory of Satan, as it was propagated at that time in the Caesar-cult, confessed the deified emperor to be the saviour of the world. The redemptive reality, which was represented by Christianity, had therefore to be regarded as a threatening rival; with brutal violence against its followers, the attempt was made to eliminate it from history.

6bWhen I saw her I marveled greatly. 7But the angel said to me, Why marvel? I will tell you the mystery of the woman, and the beast with seven heads and ten horns that carries her.

John is startled at the confusing image of the harlot Babylon and marvels how such horror is possible. The angel who showed him the vision helps him to understand it by interpreting certain details.

8The beast that you saw was, and is not, and is to ascend from the bottomless pit and go to perdition; and the dwellers of the earth whose names have not been written into the book of life from the foundation of the world, will marvel to behold the beast, because it was and is not and is to come. 9aThis calls for a mind with wisdom . . .

The explanation of the angel begins with the beast on which the woman sits; this is more thorough than the later interpretation of the figure of the harlot, although the beast has already been introduced in 13:1-10f., where its nature was identified; a sign that more attention is to be given to the beast as a more important apparition. Additional detail, which is necessary to recognize the beast each time, is here filled in; but since it had to be encoded, much of it remains obscure especially for us nowadays. John is aware of this and as in 13:18 he indicates that for understanding an insight is necessary which is not only rooted in the natural intelligence of the human being but is given as a grace to the faithful; only thus can one with certainty recognize the antichrist each time.

The first items, straight off, appears quite opaque. One thing, however, is quite clear: they are concerned with the history of the beast. It is truly a strange story; it does not quite fit into the framework within which otherwise the evolution of human existence occurs; it vacillates, rather, between two different worlds, the visible and the invisible, back and forth. The three-part statement which establishes this (". . . was, and is not, and is to ascend ") is noteworthy in that it seems to imitate the three-part predicate of God (". . . is and was and is to come "; 1 : 4). The beast, therefore, represents an attempt at imitating God; it is God's adversary whose game of opposition, however, does not quite succeed. For it is also said of it that it now " is not "; eternity which belongs to God's essence is not due to it.

This identity formula alludes to another attempt at imitation. In his manner, the antichrist would also like to imitate the first coming of Christ, his departure from the world at the ascension and his second coming for the judgment; but here again it is implied that this counter-act is only externally successful; for the parousia of the beast is not from the sphere of divine glory but from the bottomless pit of perdition, whither it must finally return for ever.

Nevertheless, the reappearance of the beast will make a great impression on those who cannot see through his nature. The elect will possess the necessary gift of discernment (cf. 13 : 8); the others, however, whose final destiny will be like that of the beast (exclusion from eternal life), confront the risen beast with astonishment (cf. 13 : 3) and reverent submission.

The meaning of this statement is not exhausted in a merely formal indication of the beast's parody of God and his Messiah; it also aims at giving in substance more accurate information concerning this apparition of the final time; at any rate, the concrete clues given here, which wisdom requires should be concealed, will only be intelligible to the insight of faith.

⁹ᵇ *. . . the seven heads are seven hills on which the woman is seated; they are also seven kings, . . .*

Continuing the interpretation, what the angel says here is so cautiously delivered that only a Christian schooled in the happenings of his time was capable of grasping its significance for contemporary history. For today's reader the contemporary history of that time would only be of significance insofar as it also contained general clues for the comprehension of final time phenomena; in addition, it would remain of special immediate interest if the author intended that the considered contemporary phenomenon be regarded as a type of some other real occurrence, which one would not have to reckon with till the last epoch of the end of time. The assumption of such a far-reaching view is supported by the multilayered nature of the apocalyptic prophecy.

At first, the seven heads are interpreted, indeed, twice over. First they represent seven hills on which the woman is sitting; the original image is transposed into another of a city which lies on seven hills. Here it is clear that the name Babylon means the city of Rome which even then was called the " seven hill city." The second interpretation fits in with the first; the seven kings would then refer to seven Roman emperors.

¹⁰ *. . . five of whom have fallen, one is, the other has not yet come, and when he comes he must remain only a little while.*

At first sight, this information gives the impression that here the first readers are offered assistance in working out the names of the emperors. If one were to attempt this nowadays, it would be best to start with the remark, " one is." As this one, who is and is sixth in the series Domitian would probably come into question since the composition of Revelation actually occurred in his reign. If one were to count back to the first, one would be faced with Caligula. Why he of all should be the first, for that there is no cogent reason. The matter gets more unreasonable when one counts forward from Domitian; then Nerva would be the last whom no human being would follow as regent save the " beast," the antichrist in person. Consequently, a purely contemporaneous interpretation proves to be if not impossible at least insufficient. In any case, the number seven alone, which is clearly used in Revelation as a symbol of completion (cf. 1:4)—whereby after the seventh member the end always comes (cf. 1:4)—forbids that the prophecy be given such a narrow framework. Evidently political power as such is in focus here inasmuch as it actively persecutes Christians; that does not exclude that apparent historical references appear here, not only to facilitate a concrete conceptualisation, but that they could also have been intended as pointers for the first readers to understand what lay immediately in store for them on the part of the Roman state.

[11]*As for the beast that was and is not, it is an eight but it belongs to the seven, and it goes to perdition.*

The whole series is geared to the eight; the main interest is focused on him in the context of the whole. As an eight he is actually supernumerary; for the seventh concluded the series of kings which is in itself complete. If, nevertheless, one counts beyond the seven this indicates, even purely formally, that something new is probably about to begin with the eight, which, on the other hand does not stand fully isolated and independent of what has just been concluded, rather, signifies its crowning fulfillment. This connection between the series of seven and the eight king is also expressly referred to: the eight " belongs to the seven " which means it is somehow already present in them.

Moreover, the connection is also symbolically noted by the fact that the seven appear as the heads of the beast. They are, therefore, related in type to it and embody it in a certain respect.

At the same time the eight appears to be of a different type to the seven. The beast has previously, in 13: 1–10, been described as an incarnation of Satan himself, as a superhuman, demonic being. In the eight, therefore, no human being appears in the same way as a representative of the antichrist, but the antichrist himself appears; the opposition to God and Christ, fermenting in the whole of the final time, points to him, the eight; he has already announced his presence in all transitory partial realizations of the anti-Christian (cf. 2 Thess. 2: 7; 1 Jn. 2: 18. 22). With his appearance before the end of the ages, hostility to God and Christ in world history will have reached its climax and its end. By virtue of his superhuman abilities and potentialities the antichrist will be able to snatch for himself universal world dominion before God finally and for ever casts him into perdition. This, his end, has been recorded here for the second time in our section (cf. v. 8); the motif of hope and encouragement runs alongside the portrayal.

[12]*And ten horns that you saw are ten kings who have not yet received royal power, but they are to receive authority as kings for one hour, together with the beast.* [13]*These are of one mind and give over their power and authority to the beast; . . .*

The ten horns of the beast (cf. 13: 1) are interpreted by the angel as representing ten kings; the same as in Daniel (7: 24) where this item comes from. These ten kings are expected to appear in the future and are in power together with the beast, but only for a short time (" one hour "), and according to God's plan, for a very special purpose which is revealed in v. 16. They prove to be loyal vassals of the beast at whose disposal they put all their might, their political, economic and military potential.

14they will make war on the Lamb, and the Lamb will conquer them, for he is Lord of lords and King of kings, and those with him are called and chosen and faithful.

With the help of these human potentates the antichrist, who himself is a demonic vassal of Satan, wages war against Christ and his faithful. Here again, as in 14:1-5, the prospect of peace flares up briefly in the midst of a hopeless situation for the Christian. In order to give comfort the angel looks ahead to the outcome of this combat which is later to be described particularly (19:11-16): Christ and his elect remain victorious against all the might of the world even though it is under the supreme command of the antichrist, the incarnate Satan. The foundation of such certainty of victory lies in the absolute: the Lord (the " Lamb "; cf. 5:1-14) raised to the throne of God must be victorious because every power outside God, even the combined forces of the whole world and of hell, fades into nothingness before God's omnipotence. In this victory, the " Lamb " will reveal himself as the " Lord of lords and the King of kings " (cf. 19:16).

15And he said to me, The waters that you saw, where the harlot is seated, are peoples and multitudes and tongues.

The interpretation of the angel now changes from the beast to the woman. The final destiny of the beast was last mentioned, hence the angel continues with the information concerning the fate of the woman, before he explains who the woman is.

The world army created in the name of the antichrist and led by him against God, Christ and the faithful, has, according to

God's decree to fulfill a contradictory task before it is annihilated. It is divine irony, if he intends and actually succeeds in using this hostile military force to execute his judgment on Babylon, the anti-Christian world capital. How extensive the power position of this metropolis is in the world, is indicated in the interpretation of the many waters (cf. Is. 8:7f.; Jer. 47:2); she holds sway over immense masses of people in the entire world (the enumeration is in the form of the cosmic number four); it surely is no accident if in the four-part enumeration here, which so often reappears in Revelation, the word " tribe " is substituted for another: " multitude," which at least in modern society is associated with the image of a mass of people of numbed self-awareness, remote-controlled and of clouded conscience.

[16]*And the ten horns that you saw, they and the beast will hate the harlot; they will make her desolate and naked, and devour her flesh and burn her up with fire, . . .*

The incredible happens: the beast, the antichrist, destroys with the aid of his vassal kings his own capital city; the harlot, which till now it has borne on its back, is gruesomely killed with diabolical hatred; God's foes mete out justice on themselves.

The description of her total annihilation seems to be somewhat mixed up (desolate—naked; devour—burn); this is because two images (city and harlot) are interchangeably used as concepts for the description.

[17]*. . . for God has put it in their hearts to carry out his purpose by being of one mind and giving over their royal power to the beast, until the words of God shall be fulfilled.*

Here the true reason for the irrational behavior of the antichrist is given. This disclosure means for the Church, which in such a world seems to be fighting a lost cause, not only great comfort, but she also receives an important lead whereby she can grasp the unintelligible contradictions which she faces in the course of history.

God alone comes positively and always to the goal with everything and everyone, even though it might happen in a wide roundabout way, sometimes even in an apparently contradictory manner. Those who think they lead are led; those who believe they command, obey. An unmasking of power is planned here whose full extent will probably strike one dumbfounded some day at the world judgment.

¹⁸And the woman that you saw is the great city which has dominion over the kings of the earth.

In conclusion of the entire section, the angel now clearly repeats the interpretation of the image of the harlot already alluded to in v. 5; what was meant was the mighty capital of the godless world which is built on a foundation laid by the Devil himself. This explains her influence on mankind. The following describes her downfall at length whose authors have already been named.

The Judgment on the World Capital Babylon (18 : 1–24)

This vision does not demonstrate the annihilation of the capital of antichrist's kingdom in a sequence of images as for instance was the case with the plagues of the three series of seven (6 : 1–11. 19; 15 : 1—6 : 21); the whole is less a visual than an auditory account. The account itself is done largely with visual material from the Old Testament but is impressively executed as an independent project. The literary production and linguistic style culminate in places in a poetic power of expression and artistic excellence.

As for content, it is to be remembered that contemporary and final history are seen all in one. Thus the Rome of the Caesars, as formerly Babylon, has become a symbol of sworn enmity against the people of God and with this against God himself and again of the quintessence of all of Satan's opposition to the Church and his war against the establishment of God's kingdom on earth.

¹After this I saw another angel coming down from heaven, having great authority; and the earth was made bright with his splendor. ²And he called out with a mighty voice, Fallen, fallen is Babylon the great! It has become a dwelling place of demons, a haunt of every foul spirit, a haunt of every foul and hateful bird; ³for all nations have drunk the wine of her impure passions, and the kings of the earth have committed fornication with her, and the merchants of the earth have grown rich with the wealth of her wantonness.

This vision is an independent vision separated formally with " after this " and as to content with the information that the bowl angel is no longer introducing it as up till now but another angel; this celestial messenger appears reflecting the glory of God who sent him (cf. Ezek. 43:2; Lk. 2:9).

The scenery is magnificent and uncanny at the same time. For the abundance of celestial light, which shines on the scene with the appearance of the angel, illumines the extensive ruins of the city sunk in ashes and nocturnal horror. No human soul is left in her, her ruins house the demons and swarms of nocturnal birds have found it a hiding place (Lev. 11:13–19 classifies all nocturnal birds and bats as unclean).

That is how Babylon looks like after she had met the fate prophesied earlier on (14:8) by an angel and described in the following. As an explanation of her lot, the angel once more reminds us of her guilt (cf. 14:8; 17:2): Babylon has seduced the whole world to defect from God, to frivolous luxury and moral collapse and thereby called down on herself God's wrath. After the outer façade has collapsed her inner foulness is laid bare. God's judgment is always also a self-judgment.

⁴Then I heard another voice from heaven saying, Come out of her my people, lest you take part in her sins, lest you share in her plagues; ⁵for her sins are heaped high as heaven, and God has remembered her iniquities. ⁶Render to her as she herself has rendered, and repay her double for her deeds; mix a double draught for her in the cup she has mixed. ⁷As she glorified herself and played the wanton, so give her a like measure of torment and mourning. Since in her heart she says, A queen I sit, I am no widow, mourning I shall never see, ⁸so shall her plagues come in a single day, pestilence and mourning and famine, and she shall be burned with fire; for mighty is the Lord God who judges her.

The introductory image of the fall of Babylon was only a prophetic forward glance; this is inferred from the summons, only now addressed to the faithful, to leave the city before the terrible catastrophe (cf. Jer. 51:6. 45; Mt. 24:15-20 par.). The explanation for this summons becomes a warning not to be infected themselves by the evil spirit of this city, not to become accessories to the crimes and consequently be condemned with her. Augustine rightly understands this summons to leave the city in a spiritual sense and explains: " We will rise and leave the city of this world on the feet of faith, active in love, and go to the living God."

The dilemma of the Christian in the world is that, on the one hand, the world is given to him as a responsibility and, on the other, he must be constantly on the alert that in the execution of his duty he does not become subject to the world by a false conformity to given realities, by obscuring the boundary between God and the world, between her spirit and the will of God (cf. Rom. 12:2). Experienced as being hitched to two repellent contrary poles, the existence of the Christian in the world can at times be felt as a painful tension, but one which must be endured unequivocally and courageously. An " exodus " must always be practiced by the Christian; without the necessary self-denial he rises with the world and falls with her, instead of proving himself her saviour in the name of Jesus Christ.

For the world capital Babylon, the residence of the antichrist, the measure of her sin as well as the measure of God's forbearance is full to overflowing. God answers her challenge, which with the sky-high mountain of her guilt can no longer be overlooked, with a merciless, just judgment. The avengers, named already in 17:16f., received the order to annihilate it root and branch and to repay her wicked deeds relentlessly even beyond the legal maxim of equality in kind and measure (cf. Jer. 16:18; 17:18). With her downfall in a single day (cf. Is. 47:8f.) the entire mendacity of her being will be laid bare, her counterfeit show of security and the hollow gesture of her absolute and universal power will crumble into dust. The alone-reigning and almighty God has passed judgment on her.

9And the kings of the earth, who committed fornication and were wanton with her, will weep and wail over her when they see the smoke of her burning; 10they will stand far off, in fear of her torment, and say, Alas! Alas! thou great city, thou mighty city Babylon! In one hour has thy judgment come. 11And the merchants of the earth weep and mourn for her, since no one buys their cargo anymore, 12cargo of gold, silver, jewels and pearls, fine linen, purple, silk and scarlet, all kinds of scented wood, all articles of ivory, all articles of costly wood, bronze, *iron and marble, *[13]*cinnamon, spice, incense, myrrh, frankin-cense, wine, oil, fine flour and wheat, cattle and sheep, horses and chariots, and slaves, that is, human souls. *[14]*The fruit for which thy soul longed has gone from thee, and all thy dainties and thy splendor are lost to thee, never to be found again! *[15]*The merchants of these wares, who gained wealth from her, will stand far off, in fear of her torment, weeping and mourning aloud, *[16]*Alas, alas, for the great city that was clothed in fine linen, in purple and in scarlet, bedecked with gold, with jewels, and with pearls! *[17a]*In one hour all this wealth has been laid waste.*

The extent and horror of the destruction is expressed, again with reference to an Old Testament model (cf. Ezek. 26:15—27:36), by means of the lamentations of those who previously knew Babylon and now, so as not to be dragged into its destruction, stand at a distance gazing at its annihilation in a fiery mass and weeping over the loss of so great riches. Like in an ancient tragedy, they give expression to their shock in three choirs.

In the first place the kings of the earth, who had sunned themselves in the favor of her world sovereignty, had dedicated life and limb to her and in payment had participated in her power and luxury (cf. 17:2; 18:3), cry out their " Alas, alas " at such a thorough destruction. However, they cannot help but admit that they are witnessing a judgment of God, while a power crumbles here which " in its colossal force, augmented to extreme limits, had become free for inappropriate hands " (Rheinhold Schneider).

The second choir is composed of the merchants of the earth who had enriched themselves from her deceptive wealth and now lament the loss of such a significant market. Not only commodities of daily life, but in her prodigal prosperity she had bought the most expensive luxury goods of a pampered way of life. The list of imported goods is revealing for clothing and adornments, beauty culture and style of living, choice of food and drink in the highly civilized society of antiquity. Not only goods, animals and utensils, which made life pleasant, comfortable and pleasurable, but also human beings which as articles one could freely dispose of, which one could use for services of any kind, were up for sale in her; trade in slaves was in this great and rich city a good source of income.

At the height of its political and economic power, Babylon, so the merchants think, would now have been able to enjoy the fruits of her prosperity; however, this expectation was not fulfilled. God avenges misused possession as he does misused power; both are equally deceptive in the hands of human beings.

[17b]*And all the shipmasters and seafaring men, sailors and all whose trade is on the sea, stood far off* [18]*and cried out as they saw the smoke of her burning, What city was like the great city?* [19]*And they threw dust on their heads, as they wept and mourned, crying out, Alas, alas, for the great city where all who had ships at sea grew rich by her wealth! In one hour she had been laid waste.*

As a third group, the seafaring men lament her destruction: shipowners and captains, helmsmen and sailors; all who lived by sea-voyages and worked in the harbors. The proud city into whose harbor sailed a mass of large and small ships each richly laden is no more. Of course their sadness, like that of the merchants, is not really selfless; like the latter they lament the annihilation of the source of their own prosperity.

All three groups are especially stricken by the fact, which they emphasize each time at the end of their lament, that such a fate should so suddenly and unexpectedly strike the capital of the world and that she should be reduced to rubble and ashes in an instant. Security is one of the most primitive and urgent desires of the human heart; the greatest possible assurance against all accidents of existence motivates modern thought and people are willing to pay much for it. But life itself remains finally insecure because of one factor which remains beyond any calculation; it is God in whom " we live and move and have our being " (Acts 17:28). The spirit of Babylon with the one-sidedness of its horizontal existence and its idolization of transitory values will despite its denial always be judged and one day finally and conclusively by the vertical.

²⁰*Rejoice over her, O Heaven, O saints and apostles and prophets, for God has given judgment for you against her!*

The celestial voice, which let John hear the lamentations of the dwellers on earth over Babel's fall, imparts to him in conclusion the judgment of heaven on the event. This is clothed in the form of a call on heaven to exchange the lamentations on earth for hymns of joy. All inhabitants of heaven, especially the apostles and prophets, the preachers of true salvation to the world, are summoned for this, for now God has heard the prayers of the martyrs (6:9-11) by aiding truth and righteousness to victory. Before heaven returns an answer in the form of an especially solemn liturgy of thanksgiving (19:1-10), the judgment vision on the fall of Babylon is first brought to an end.

²¹*Then a mighty angel took up a stone like a great millstone and threw it into the sea, saying, So shall Babylon the great city be thrown down with violence, and shall be found no more; ²²and the sound of harpers and minstrels, of flute players and trum- peters, shall be heard in thee no more; the voice of bridegroom and bride shall be heard in thee no more; ²³for thy merchants were the great men of the earth, and all nations were deceived*

by thy sorcery. [24]And in her was found the blood of prophets and saints, and all who have been slain on earth.

With a symbolic action, whose model is found in Jer. 51:60–64, the angel illustrates what remains of Babylon after God's judgment. Nothing, she sank in an instant, completely and for ever, just as the large stone which he throws into the sea.

How absolutely desolate the metropolis of the antichrist will be after God's judgment is illustrated by further images. In the epic-type description of the desolate city many Old Testament motifs reappear. All signs of life have vanished. No human voice, no song, no musical instrument can be heard, altogether a depressing silent emptiness (cf. Is. 24:8; Ezek. 26:13). All the sounds of the former workday and the industry of its inhabitants have ceased; there is no household, no handicraft anymore in Babylon. A certain sadness at how many genuine values of human life have sunk even with Babylon can be detected in this elegy. Wholesome joy has also died with the wanton frenzy of life; no young man speaks lovingly to the bride of his heart; there are no more new families established; no children born. And over the dead silence of this field of ruins dark night reigns for ever.

Jubilation in Heaven and on Earth at God's Judgment on Babylon (19: 1–10)

[1]*After this I heard what seemed to be the mighty voice of a great multitude in heaven, crying, Hallelujah! Salvation and power and glory belong to our God, [2]for his judgments are true and just; he has judged the great harlot who corrupted the earth with her fornication, and he has avenged on her the blood of his servants. [3]Once more they cried, Hallelujah! The smoke from her goes up for ever and ever. [4]And the twenty-four elders*

and the four living creatures fell down and worshipped God who is seated on the throne, saying, Amen. Hallelujah!

John raises his eyes from the desolate Babylon to heaven. There the blessed spirits, together with the transfigured human beings who have already achieved their eternal goal, celebrate the overthrow of the residence of the antichrist in hymns of victory. Thanksgiving for this is offered in three successive choirs to him who sits on the throne, the Almighty; every choir begins with a cry of joy, Hallelujah (" praise the Lord ") which had been taken over from the temple liturgy at Jerusalem, presumably by the young community at Jerusalem and like the Amen has from there entered Christian liturgy untranslated as an acclamation; moreover, the Hallelujah is found here for the first time in a Christian document and for the only time in the New Testament. The heavenly choirs base their praise of God on the fact that with the judgment on the harlot God has now revealed himself as just; she was the center of infection which corrupted the world and the real mainspring of all bloody persecutions against Christians. The cry Hallelujah is repeated and newly motivated with the explanation that this " true and just " judgment of God is irrevocable and eternal (cf. 14:11); the final and complete redemption appears thereby at the horizon of world-history. The elders and the living creatures on their part take up the cry of joy with a gesture of worship and substantiate the hymn of praise of the blessed angels and men with Amen (cf. 4:10f.; 5:8. 14; 7:9–12; 11:16; 14:3).

⁵And from the throne came a voice crying, Praise our God, all you his servants, you who fear him small and great. ⁶Then I heard what seemed to be the voice of a great multitude, like the sound of many waters and like the sound of mighty thunder-peals, crying, Hallelujah! For the Lord our God the Almighty reigns. ⁷Let us rejoice and exult and give him glory, for the marriage of the Lamb has come, and his bride has made herself ready; ⁸it was granted her to be clothed in fine linen, bright and pure—for the linen is the righteous deeds of the saints.

The third Hallelujah roars even mightier up towards the Almighty; a choir of a vast multitude sounds like the united voices of the loudest natural forces like the roar of mighty waterfalls and the clap of heavy thunder.

The summons from the vicinity of the throne—presumably from one of the living creatures (" our God "!)—has now been answered by all the servants of God on earth, the entire Church of God which has not yet arrived at the eternal goal, all the faithful without distinction of rank and status; no one is small or superfluous before God. The Church of God on earth rejoices and thanks God above all because in judgment he now sweeps aside what stood in the way of the perfect establishment of his reign on earth. With the fall of Babylon he has begun his final great work of bringing his creation to perfection and the history of mankind to its goal.

Still a further reason for jubilation is mentioned: The hour of the marriage of the Lamb has arrived; it is later described in detail (21:9ff.). The image goes back to an idea of the Old Testament prophets where the relation of God to his people is viewed in analogy to the union between man and woman in marriage. Jesus uses the image of the marriage feast in various ways to illustrate the completion of redemption. The personal relationship which exists between him and the redeemed is comparable to the relationship between bridegroom and bride (cf. 2 Cor. 11:2; Eph. 5:25–33).

When the Christians on earth who are tested by suffering explain, " the marriage of the Lamb has come," that is the same as to say, the promise of their Lord's second coming is being fulfilled. He is coming to bring his Church home from exile into his glory. When the entire Church on earth is united with Christ, her heavenly bridegroom, then the aim of his redemptive work is fully achieved.

Ready in her bridal dress, the Church waits expectantly and longingly to receive her Lord. Her bridal dress is a gift from God (" it was granted her "; cf. 6 : 2), he himself has clothed her in his grace. The dress is simple, but genuine and noble in comparison with the obtrusive adornments of her counterpart the harlot Babylon (cf. 17 : 4); the whiteness is a symbol of sanctity and of the transfiguration which awaits her in the glory of God.

In a concluding explanation a second mark of origin is given for the bridal dress. It has already been explained as a gift of God's grace; here we are told that it is also woven out of the good works of the Christians. At the root of this thought is the same relationship between grace and good works as is recorded more clearly by Paul in Phil. 2 : 12–14. The " how " of the joint operation between the free grace of God and the free co-operation of man remains a mystery because God himself is directly involved (cf. Eph. 2 : 10). The moral exhortation which is implied in this assertion cannot be ignored; every Christian is here set the task of collaboration with his good deeds in the weaving of the wedding dress of the Church and to enhance its beauty.

[9]*And the angel said to me, Write this : Blessed are those who are invited to the marriage supper of the Lamb. And he said to me, These are true words of God.* [10]*Then I fell down at his feet to worship him, but he said to me, You must not do that! I am a fellow servant with you and your brethren who hold the testimony of Jesus. Worship God. For the testimony of Jesus is the spirit of prophecy.*

The song of jubilation, with which the Church on earth has joined in, still lies in the future for the addressees of Revelation; in the meantime it is for them only an expression of hope for which they live and are willing to die. Hence the forward glimpse of the consummation concludes with a beatitude of those who are called to the marriage feast (cf. Lk. 14:15). The promise aims at arousing confidence, energy as well as courage in suffering for the time of persecution. For this purpose a special attestation follows.

As improbable as this prospect might sound to human ears and as incomprehensible as it may remain for the understanding it is, nevertheless, trustworthy; the angel explains that what John has seen and heard were the words of God's revelation which bear the stamp of the truthfulness and dependability of God himself.

Still quite confused and affected by this vision of the future and the impression of the angel's last words, John forgets whom he has before him. Worshipping, he falls at the feet of the angel who energetically rebuffs him because only to God alone is due this type of veneration. He introduces himself as one who like John and the other Christian prophets (" who hold the testimony of Jesus "; cf. 1:5) is employed in God's service. Indirectly, John once more receives thereby a confirmation of his prophetic calling; the " testimony of Jesus " himself is audible in what he offers the Church in this document (cf. 1:1). The testimony of Jesus lives on and unfolds in the words with which the Spirit inspires men called to prophetic propagation (cf. Jn. 14:26; 15:26f.); the Spirit of God is indeed also the Spirit of Jesus (cf. Jn. 16:13f.; Rom. 8:9; 2 Cor. 3:17).

Propagation which has not Christ at its root and does not pass on its testimony in the Holy Spirit is not Christian propagation.

THE RETURN OF CHRIST AND
THE FINAL JUDGMENT (19:11—20:15)

The Judgment on the Beast and His Followers
(19:11–21)

The execution of the judgment on the anti-Christian world
capital was by God's decree (cf. 17 : 16f.) allotted to the antichrist
and his confederates. Christ himself appears at the judgment of
the antichrist, of his associates and followers (19 : 11–21). After
that, their task-master Satan will be stripped of his power on
earth (20 : 1–6) and finally will be banished from God's creation
for ever (20 : 7–10). The obstructive factor in God's history of
salvation with mankind is thereby removed, the final renewal
can now begin (20 : 11–15).

The Apparition of the Logos-Rider (19 : 11–16)

It is the vision of the parousia of Christ; the scene is internally
closely linked to many previous portrayals; the person of the
judge and the court itself had often been referred to; as motifs
in the exposition as a whole, they play the role of foundation
and corner stone in a building.

Already in 12 : 1–12 the Messiah was introduced as victor over
the dragon and lord of the world; for the time being his victory
remained concealed in world-history. It seemed, on the contrary,
as if God's adversary is the true lord of the world. Section 12 :
13–17 was generally about this; the image 13 : 1–18 added greater
detail and single items to the subject.

Just as the Redeemer appeared at his first advent in the form of a helpless new-born infant, which seemed to be at the mercy of the dragon, so the inner reality of the redeemed world in the time between his ascension and return remains concealed to external perception. It was only recognized by, and present to Christ's faithful in faith who by virtue of this faith clung to this truth in the face of the contrary experiences of history. The epoch of provisionality in history has now expired. In the revelation of the glory of their exalted Lord at the parousia, the faithful see what till now they had believed.

The judgment over which their returned Lord presides was already announced in detail in 14:6–13 and subsequently depicted in its double aspect as a happening of salvation and perdition (14:14–20; cf. also 16:14; 17:14). Hence the depiction of the actual occurrence of the event can be kept relatively short.

[11]*Then I saw heaven opened, and behold, a white horse! He who sat upon it is called Faithful and True, and in righteousness he judges and makes war.*

For the third time John sees the heavens opening (cf. 4:1; 11:19); from now on it will close no more. For he whom the Seer sees entering the world from heaven will not leave it again as he did at the ascension after his resurrection.

The portrayal does not begin with the person of the rider but that of his mount (as also 4:2 and 14:14). Here a white horse has taken the place of a white cloud (cf. 14:14) the usual sign for the advent of the judge; in the framework of our image the judge indeed appears as a military leader who triumphs over his foes (19:19–21). As in other places, the gleaming white suggests affiliation to the transfigured world of heaven (cf. 3:4f. 18; 4:4; 6:11 and often).

The appearance of the rider is not at first described, rather by details of his nature and his actions his inner being is revealed. Two characteristics (" Faithful and True "), which proclaim his essence in the form of a name, are first mentioned; the Son of Man in the vocation-vision (1 : 12–20) was introduced (1 : 5; 3 : 14) with the same characteristics. There as here, they referred to the dependability of his words and promises. His return manifests that the faithful did not depend on him, and remain firm in persecution in vain. The name formula describes concisely in the form of a profession the relationship of Christ to his Church on earth, while the subsequent pronouncement concerning his actions as judge expounds his attitude to his foes in the world who had so far given the deceptive impression of invincibility (cf. 13 : 4). In Isaiah there is a prophecy of the Messiah that " with righteousness he shall judge " (Is. 11 : 3–5); now he appears to champion the rights of his faithful in the face of opponents.

12His eyes are a flame of fire, and on his head are many diadems; and he has a name inscribed which no one knows but himself.

These brief remarks concerning his appearance are not new. In 1 : 14 we found the same image which ascribes to the Son of Man the gaze of omniscience illuminating and penetrating everything. The symbols of sovereignty are not limited as in case of the dragon (12 : 3) and his image and likeness (13 : 1); the rider on the white horse is almighty. The unuttered name which declares his essence and which he alone grasps (cf. 2 : 17) is adequately indicated by these references; it is " the name which is above all names " (Phil. 2 : 9); when he appears " we shall see him as he is " (1 Jn. 3 : 2) and the secret of his being will be revealed; then he will also externally appear as he who always was, as the Son of God.

¹³He is clad in a robe dipped in blood, and the name by which he is called is the Word of God.

Christ comes out of the glory of heaven with a garment soaked in blood. This prohibits the interpretation of this trait in line with the image of the man who trod the wine press (Is. 63:1–4), which is alluded to in 14:20 in the proclamation of the judgment on the wicked, but in this context not till 19:15. If Christ brings the bloody robe with him from heaven before he has held judgment, then the blood on the robe can only be his own; and the image conveys the same as one we have already met: " a lamb as though it had been slain " (5:6), which in 5:9 was expressly interpreted to mean the death of Jesus as the cause of redemption. Accordingly, the image conveys here that the judge of the world is also its redeemer; the office of judge is his precisely because of the deed of redemption.

The third name of the rider, " the Word of God," fits also into this vantage point. It is not the case here of a name previously withheld in v. 12 and now being revealed. The Logos title is known from the Prologue of John's Gospel (Jn. 1:1–18); nevertheless, it should not without further ado be explained and understood as it is understood in that text. In the context here it is more heavily underlined than there as the name of a function and is meant to remind us that he who returns as judge was first of all sent into the world as a messenger of revelation who bore witness to God not only in words but also, and above all, in his person and in his life. Thus in the last two items the relationship is highlighted which exists between the judge and humanity as a whole and especially between him and those who in faith have preserved the " witness of Jesus " (cf. 6:9; 12:17). With the parousia their faith is fully and perfectly attested, the " word of God " is now manifest as " Faithful and True " before the whole world.

*¹⁴And the armies of heaven, arrayed in fine linen, white and
pure, followed him on white horses.*

In Biblical imagery of judgment heavenly armies as followers
of the judge have a fixed place (Mk. 13:27 par.; Mt. 25:31;
2 Thess. 1:7f.); to begin with, angelic hosts are referred to, but
according to 1 Cor. 6:2 the blessed human beings also take part
in the judgment.

*¹⁵From his mouth issues a sharp sword with which to smite
nations, and he will rule them with a rod of iron; he will tread
the wine press of the fury of the wrath of God the Almighty.*

In the characterization of the coming judge, his relationship
to the faithful has received special attention so far; this is now
continued with special reference to the " nations," that is, the
ungodly. As judge, Christ brings not only the history of his
Church but also the entire world to its termination and fulfillment.

Three Old Testament images which have all been used in
earlier texts (cf. 1:16; 2:27; 12:5; 14:19f.) depict Christ as the
Lord and Judge of the heathens. His word of judgment immediately transforms the sentence like a sharp sword into deed; it
strikes the condemned like a blow with an iron rod.

*¹⁶On his robe and on his thigh he has a name inscribed, King
of kings and Lord of lords.*

In conclusion, the name is announced which establishes the
omnipotence of the judge and explains the impotence of those
judged. The name is on his thigh, a place especially conspicuous
in a horseman; the name tallies with the one already given to
the Lamb in the prediction of his victory (17:14) and expresses

here as there that the judge appears with the omnipotence of God, that at the parousia he appears also to his foes as he who was and is, almighty, like God himself.

The Annihilation of the Beast and His Confederates (19 : 17–21)

[17]*Then I saw an angel standing in the sun, and with a loud voice he called to all the birds that fly in midheaven, Come gather for the great supper of God,* [18]*to eat the flesh of kings, the flesh of captains, the flesh of mighty men, the flesh of horses and their riders, and the flesh of all men both free and slave, both small and great.*

As in the prelude of a drama, the summons of the angel here hints at the outcome in advance. He stands in the light of the sun (cf. 12:1) and summons all the carrion birds which fly high in the heavens to attend a gruesome banquet of corpses which God prepares for them. The picture copies a description by Ezekiel (Ezek. 39:17-20) and is here contrasted as a shocking counterpiece with the marriage feast of the Lamb to which the elect are invited (19:7–9).

[19]*And I saw the beast and the kings of the earth with their armies gathered to make war against him who sits upon the horse and against his army.* [20]*And the beast was captured, and with it the false prophet who in its presence had worked the signs by which he deceived those who had received the mark of the beast and those who worshipped its image. These two were thrown alive into the lake of fire that burns with brimstone.* [21]*And the rest were slain by the sword of him who sits upon the horse, the sword that issues from his mouth; and all the birds were gorged with their flesh.*

After the announcement, the fulfillment follows in a second image. Referring back to an allusion to the gathering of all the kings of the earth at the judgment already made in 16:14, the triumph of the Logos-rider over all his foes is merely established. The battle has long ago been fought at the death of Jesus and decided in victory through his resurrection (cf. 12:5–12). Hence we find not a trace here of combat; all the forces summoned in the name of the antichrist already lie dead on the ground to the last man. When the "lion of the tribe of Judah" (5:5) is revealed to the world as the one who has long since been victorious then only the consequences of his victory need be drawn for world-history. This happens without effort or expenditure. Those who seemed to be almighty on earth, whose corruptive activity and world-wide influence is once more called to mind (cf. 13:11–18), permit themselves to be captured as if paralyzed. The two beasts are taken back from whence they came and thrown into hell to eternal torment (cf. 14:10f.; 20:10, 14f.; 21:8). The almighty judge pronounces the death-sentence on their followers which is immediately executed. The eternal fate of the beast worshippers is referred to again later (20:15; 21:8).

The Judgment on Satan (20:1–10)

The judgment on the beast and his followers has taken from Satan the instruments with whose aid he had successfully worked to establish on earth a counter-kingdom to the kingdom of God founded by Christ and its interim historical, visible form, the Church. To continue with this plan, he is once more completely left to his own resources. In addition, his own situation has totally changed since the parousia (19:11-16). His position was already a losing one since the redemptive act of Christ (cf. 12:7–12). Yet despite the transformed reality of man and world through the life of Jesus (cf. 12:9–11), a respite was left him to continue his mischief on earth (12:12). The reprieve has expired. The illusionary power with which Satan was able to make a show in history till now is unmasked as such for all the world to see and, indeed, this happens still within history and on the ground of the old world. The concealed reality of salvation which was already known and present to the believer will therefore be visibly manifest one day in the course of world history and not just at its termination. This basic thought as leitmotiv seems to determine the not easily comprehensible exposition concerning the binding of Satan, the millennium, and the subsequent short-lived release of the Devil.

The Binding of Satan; the Millennium (20:1–6)

¹*Then I saw an angel coming down from heaven, holding in his hand the key of the bottomless pit and a great chain.*

In a new vision which is not linked with the Logos-rider, John sees an angel from heaven coming down to earth. The objects which he carries indicate his task. Christ is the keeper of the " key of the bottomless pit " (cf. 1:18); it had been handed to a fallen angel (9:1) who was to unleash the fifth trumpet plague by opening the bottomless pit (cf. 9:1f.). The angel of God, however, was not sent to let the demons loose but to lock in their supreme commander; this is indicated by the chain which he carries with him.

²*And he seized the dragon, the ancient serpent, who is the Devil and Satan, and bound him for a thousand years, . . .*

The angel fulfills his task without effort; as if impotent, the dragon must allow himself to be fettered, for despite his dangerousness, which was depicted earlier on in horrifying images, he had been made harmless long ago. The repetition of the characterization from 12:9 is intended less as a reminder and explanation of his threatening intentions and actions than of a successful victory over them (12:7–9), for which reason the execution of his task is so easy for the angel.

This unmasking scene acquires its special import if one considers it from the viewpoint of Revelation's basic hortative intention. It establishes simply and obviously the illusionary nature of the power of God's adversary for him who confronts him in the name of God so that the faithful can face him without fear and with absolute security.

The image of the binding of Satan is an age-old motif which can be found in the mythology of almost all peoples, but was of special significance in religions based on dualism like the Persian: the binding of the destructive power of evil felt everywhere in nature and in history.

[3] . . . *and threw him into the pit, and shut it and sealed it over him, that he should deceive the nations no more, till the thousand years were ended. After that he must be loosened for a little while.*

The banishment of Satan out of history, which God has decreed, he guarantees (the seal of God on the door-lock!) for a space of a thousand years, that is, for a relatively long time. During this epoch the Devil has no direct influence on the events in the world and must leave mankind in peace.

With a forward glimpse of 20:7–10 we find here already an indication of what will happen after the appointed time has expired: after that he "must," that is, by God's decree, be left free for a short while for the last time; not till then will the final judgment be pronounced on him.

'Then I saw thrones, and seated on them were those to whom judgment was committed. Also I saw the souls of those who had been beheaded for their testimony to Jesus and for the word of God, and who had not worshipped the beast and its image and had not received its mark on their foreheads or their hands. They came to life and reigned with Christ a thousand years. ⁵The rest of the dead did not come to life till the thousand years were ended. This is the first resurrection.

We look in vain for any account of what it will be like on earth during the Millennium. The vision which says something directly about it takes place in heaven. It represents a court sitting. Who the judges are is of no importance for the instruction which this vision means to impart; so they remain unnamed. Two separate groups on whom judgment is to be pronounced appear before the court. The first group consists of martyrs who were already in 6:9 characterized in the same way; the second group consists of confessors who have kept their faith in the time of the antichrist (cf. 13:8, 15–17; 15:2) without having had to testify to it with their blood. The judges in heaven promise both groups the reward of a new life after death which involves, as already stated (5:10), a share in the reign of Christ over the world (cf. 2:26f.; 3:21).

The limitation of their rule to the time of Satan's banishment out of this world is not easy to understand at first sight. The vision presents a picture from heaven; it is, therefore, also to be regarded as the place where the co-rulers with Christ are stationed. Moreover, it is clearly implied that their present reward is not the final one; it is, rather, concerned with giving information about their appointed lot during the "thousand years." It would seem to be of decisive importance for the correct understanding of the whole to discover what meaning is here ascribed to the statement: "they came to life." The resurrection of the body is not expected till later, immediately after the final judgment (v. 13), and it involves the wicked as well as the good (cf. v. 12 and v. 15). As for the " rest of the dead "—in the context this refers to the followers of the beast—it is expressly stated that they remain dead. A twofold bodily resurrection of the good is inconceivable and would in itself be nonsensical. The " first resurrection " can, therefore, refer only to a transcendental reality, that is to say, a factor which exists above earthly reality but is not without significance for it and influence on it. The vision itself indicates this circumstance in that it takes place in heaven, not on earth. All things considered, there remains only one sensible interpretation: The " first resurrection " is a participation in the glory and with this a share in the reign of the transfigured Christ. These are granted to those who have sacrificed their lives for their confession of Christ and those also who without martyrdom but faith in him have walked through the gates of death into true life; their " first death " became their " first resurrection." The " second death " awaits all the rest after the " first death " (cf. 19:21) as we read in the next verse; what this means is not explained till later (20:14).

Blessed and holy is he who shares in the first resurrection! Over such, the second death has no power, but they shall be priests of God and of Christ, and they shall reign with him a thousand years.

The beatitude names the saints who share in the first resurrection; in the original meaning of the word it signifies that they, divorced from evil, are taken into the transcendental sphere of God and exist in a living fellowship with him whose essence is holiness. Because of their new mode of existence the " second death " cannot touch them; they remain preserved from eternal damnation (cf. 2:11).

Hence the " first resurrection " and the " second death " are mutually exclusive. The " second death " refers to the condition of the damned; this leads one to assume that the " first resurrection " is the contrary condition, namely, the blessed union with Christ in the glory of the Father. In this fits the following description of the blessed life as a priestly service for God and Christ and as a reigning with the Redeemer of the world (cf. 1:6 and 5:10) on the throne of the Father (cf. 3:21).

From this one can infer something of the conditions and the state of the Church on earth during the time in which Satan has no power. During this time he can utilize neither demonic nor human instruments to wage war against the people of God (cf. 19:20; 20:3). The epoch of struggle for the Church is followed by a time of peace from the outside as well as the inside. The reign of Christ and his saints, their triumph in heaven, will then also be correspondingly reflected on earth in the constitution of human society as such, as well as in its individual groupings. After the influence of demonic power in history has been eliminated the situation which results from this on earth can in a spiritual sense be conceived as a seizure of power by Christ and his saints; the propagation of the gospel among mankind would go on undisturbed and its influence on human society remain unimpeded.

Of course the fettering of the Devil does not mean that evil has been fully eliminated from mankind. The other source of evil, the human heart, for " the imagination of the human heart is evil from its youth " (Gen. 8:21), remains. Wickedness and sin as well as misfortune and death will not vanish from the world even during this earthly epoch of peace for the Church; the earth has not yet been restored to its original paradisiacal state.

The Final Fall of Satan (20 :7–10)

[7]And when the thousand years are ended, Satan will be loosed from his prison [8]and will come out to deceive the nations which are at the four corners of the earth, that is, Gog and Magog, to gather them for battle; their number is like the sand of the sea.

What was already announced in v. 3 as part of the divine plan of history, the loosening of Satan, is now briefly executed. He immediately grasps the proffered opportunity to intervene in history after his fashion and bring about confusion. By being made powerless himself for a while, as well as by the final defeat of his associates, the beasts, he had been impeded in his earlier intention and activity " to deceive the nations "; now he applies himself alone to the task of rallying to his side the political powers of the world and inciting them against " the camp of the saints and the beloved city " (cf. 14:1–5), that is to say, against the followers of Christ and his Church. He succeeds in instigating a general rebellion (" at the four corners of the earth "; the cosmic number of completion: four); the masses which gather together for the second levy of Satan are in-numerable—which is what the traditional biblical simile " like the sand of the sea " means—and under his command they prepare for the last onslaught against the people of God. As to content and execution, this picture was inspired by and relies on the model which is executed at great length in Ezekiel 38: 1—39:20. There too we find the mythological names Gog and Magog which were already utilized in Jewish apocalyptic litera-ture as symbolic names for the hostile masses which are mobil-ized for battle against the Messianic kingdom of the final time from the four corners of the earth.

[9]And they marched up over the broad earth and surrounded the

camp of the saints and the beloved city; but fire came down from heaven and consumed them, [10]*and the Devil who had deceived them was thrown into a lake of fire and brimstone where the beast and the false prophet were, and they will be tormented day and night for ever and ever.*

Once again the situation of the Church seems quite hopeless against such a powerful army which has surrounded and laid siege to her. For the second time the whole contingent of God's foes, who wish to contest the reign of God and his Messiah on earth, are gathered together in one place (cf. 16:14-16; 19: 17-21). As in the first instance no battle takes place; God miraculously intervenes to help his " beloved city " by consuming the super-power of the enemy in an instant with fire from heaven (cf. Ezek. 38:22).

With this last attempt the " mystery of lawlessness " (2 Thess. 2:6) is fully revealed in its dreadfulness and, at the same time, in its impotence in the course of world history; the defeat of Satan which has already been achieved (cf. 12:7-11) becomes now historically manifest. The short time, in which he was permitted once more to give full vent to the wrath of one already damned against the Church of God on earth (cf. 12:12), has now expired; corresponding to his essence of radical negation of God and everything that belongs to him his exclusion from the world of God now becomes final and eternal and this separation from God ends in eternal misery. The Satanic trinity, after a short and frenzied show of force, is once more together powerless in the eternal torment of the wicked. He who has chosen to follow Satan has done so, like the followers of Christ, for all eternity.

The Last Judgment (20:11–15)

¹¹Then I saw a great white throne and him who sat upon it; from his presence earth and sky fled away, and no place was found for them.

With Satan there has been removed from God's creation the real factor of disturbance and destruction, the final cause of all chaotic processes in world history. Hence the most important pre-condition for the possibility of a new ordering of the world, its transition into the final state of consummation, has been established.

Like the entire series of images concerning the future, the last act of world history is introduced with a throne vision (cf. 4:1—5:14); this sign of God's sovereignty was placed at the beginning of the disclosures concerning world and salvation history, with the same sign the whole is brought to a full stop. All the judgments of God in the course of history, especially those described in the three series of plagues, had for final aim to re-establish a disturbed order. In the last judgment the disorder of injustice, which has infected all areas of life in the course of world history, is completely and for ever rectified by the absolute righteousness of a final, all-compensating divine judgment. Creation, which had been drawn into suffering by man's sin, affected by the curse on it, and brought into confusion by the influence of evil (cf. Gen. 3:17), will pass away in its deformed state when the glory of the all-holy God shines upon it at his advent in judgment. This termination of the world which is delineated at length in the synoptic apocalypse (cf. Mk. 13:24–27 par.) is here drawn with only a few lines but all the more forcefully and memorably.

Heaven and earth have passed away; all that remains is the symbol of judgment, the great throne commanding the whole picture in the shining white of God's glory. As in 4:2, the enthroned is not mentioned by name; the sameness of the images in 4:2 and 20:11 leads one to conclude that it is the same person; accordingly, the Father appears here as the judge of the world. This monumental picture, which retains only the essentials for the sake of a stronger impression, does not exclude the idea that the Father holds judgment through his Son, of which there is ample testimony (cf. 6:16f.; 14:14f.; Jn. 5:22).

[12]*And I saw the dead, great and small, standing before the throne, and books were opened. Also another book was opened, which is the book of life. And the dead were judged by what was written in the books, by what they had done.* [13]*And the sea gave up the dead in it, Death and Hades gave up the dead in them, and all were judged by what they had done.*

All at once John sees all the dead standing before the throne of judgment; no one who ever lived, wherever he may have been buried, is missing; land and water, Death and Hades, presented as personified powers as in 6:8, can keep no one back for themselves.

The fact of the judgment and the yardstick applied are meant to be clarified and emphatically stressed by this compressed account. For this purpose only the process of judgment gets longer treatment and the striking reversal of judgment and awakening of the dead have the same purpose. Before the Judge there is no respect of persons; the same yardstick is applied to all; everyone stands alone before God; from his lips issues the final and the one and only fully and quite objective judgment on every human being and his work. The description lays its main stress on this special circumstances; with the aid of an impressive image of the books consulted for the judgment this thought is commandingly shifted into the center.

Two types of book give the necessary information. One type is present in many exemplars; evidently there is a book of his own for everyone who is judged. The second type on the other hand is present only in one copy; it contains the list of names, the list of heavenly citizens; we have already heard about it, it is called the " book of life (3:5; 17:8) or the " book of life of the Lamb " (13:8; 21:27). This register serves as the first supporting document for the judgment.

Besides this, one other book is important for the judgment, the record of what everyone has done in his life, the book of his " works " (cf. Dan. 7:10). Election and works, grace and co-operation, calling and its personal fulfillment must tally if the judgment is to be positive. The final judgment, therefore, is nought but the universal disclosure of the decision everybody has made for himself (cf. Jn. 3:18f.).

Then Death and Hades were thrown into the lake of fire. This is the second death, the lake of fire; and if anyone's name was not found written in the book of life, he was thrown into the lake of fire.

With the final judgment " this age " (Mt. 12:32; Lk. 16:8; 20:34; Rom. 12:2) has expired, the " present evil age " (Gal. 1:4) must make way for the " age to come " (Mt. 12:32; Eph. 1:21; 2:7 and often). Two powers of " this age " who owe their existence to sin (cf. Rom. 5:12–21) and have yet to be eliminated are specially mentioned: Death and Hades. They are excluded from God's creation as the " last enemy " (1 Cor. 15:26) before life can celebrate in it its eternal triumph. The two powers are once more personified, indeed, they are imagined as demonic beings, because as phenomena resulting from sin they have ravaged and reversed the shape of God's creation. Hence they are also sent into perdition with Satan and his accomplices, where those human beings who did not pass God's judgment are also to be found.

The hopeless condition of the damned in eternal torment (cf. 20:10) Revelation calls the "second death," from which there is no resurrection.

THE CONSUMMATION (21:1—22:5)

The "ruler of this world" was already judged at the first coming of Christ (cf. 12:7-12; Jn. 16:11). Notwithstanding this, he was able with God's permission (cf. 13:7) in an historical interim period (cf. 12:12) to make the despairing attempt to assert himself in the position of power he had up till then; world history was brought by this into considerable confusion and the effects of the redemptive act of Christ on the state of human society were severely impeded.

With the return of Christ the situation has changed. The associates of Satan and their followers had already been apprehended (cf. 19:20); they no longer have any influence on the course of world history. After a last vain attempt (cf. 20:7-9), a definite end was put to the activity of Satan himself; his place is now not on earth but for ever in the lake of fire (cf. 20:10). The old world which had been very involved in the suffering wrought by sin and its consequences is dissolved (cf. 20:11); among human beings the separation of good and evil has been accomplished in the final judgment (cf. 20:12-15).

The purification of world history in the world judgment and the dissolution of the old cosmos were intended to create space for the new creation and the new mankind. The images which are still to come are all inspired by the leitmotiv: "Behold, I make all things new" (v. 5).

Through the act of redemption the "Lamb, as though it had been slain" (5:6), had already energetically taken the destiny of God's world under his control; this victory of the "lion of the tribe of Judah" (5:5) is now made manifest in its full consequences. The new world without a shadow of imperfection and transitoriness is making its appearance; the new mankind without sin and consequently without any want emerges.

Introductory Vision (21: 1–8)

¹Then I saw a new heaven and a new earth; for the first heaven and the first earth had passed away, and the sea was no more. ²And I saw the holy city, new Jerusalem, coming down out of heaven from God, prepared as a bride adorned for her husband; . . .

The first two verses solemnly announce the climax of the entire book, the consummation of God's secret (cf. 10:7); the wording relies closely on prophetic utterances of the Old Testament (cf. Is. 65; also 66:22). Like a heading they announce the theme of the last vision of the book: the new world and the new Jerusalem.

The delineation of this vision does not begin till v. 9; a long introduction (21:3–8), also in the form of a vision, has been put in front to render prominent the importance and significance of the subsequent pictorial account and in the manner of a prologue to give a forward glimpse of its meaningful content.

A completely new earth has taken the place of the old world and a new heaven is stretched over it (cf. Gen. 1:1); nothing remains of the first creation. It is noteworthy that special reference is made to the sea having vanished; it was considered to be the last remains of the original chaos (cf. Gen. 1:2; also 1:1).

The essential form of the new world is the heavenly Jerusalem. God's heaven gives it concrete shape; the human and divine spheres of existence are now wholly intertwined; earth and heaven are now one. What this purports and signifies is illustrated in greater detail with the aid of Old Testament pictorial concepts.

The entire cosmos is incorporated into the heaven of God, pictorially represented as a coming down of the holy city of God to earth (cf. 3:12). She bears the symbolic name: "The new Jerusalem." She has only something in common with the old Jerusalem on earth, the temple city of the old Covenant, insofar as the presence of God revealed in a cloud in the holy of holies of the temple has now from being a mere symbol acquired full reality; the Old Testament sign of promise has been fulfilled. This has not happened in the manner of a transformation of the old Jerusalem, an eternalization of its transfigured form; something completely new has taken its place: "The new Jerusalem" is in its essence a transcendental reality which has existed with God from eternity.

In the second image, that of the bride, this new Jerusalem is related to the Church of Jesus Christ. The image of the followers of the Lamb on Mount Zion (14:1-5) had represented the Church as a holy community in its union by grace with its transfigured Lord on the inside but in the conditions of the old earth; now on the new earth her inner wealth and her supernatural beauty are expressed even in its external form; in the new creation reality the people of God celebrate "the marriage of the Lamb" (cf. 19:7).

[3] . . . *and I heard a great voice from the throne saying, Behold the dwelling of God is with men. He will dwell with them, and they shall be his people, and God himself will be with them; . . .*

With two groups of sayings, again wholly fashioned from Old Testament words and images, the new reality is still further illustrated.

The first speaker, " a great voice from the throne " (cf. 19:5), explains that the promise given to the first Covenant people of a new and perfect life-fellowship with God is now fulfilled. What tabernacle and temple had represented in type and meant as hope to the people of Israel has happened; God has opened the holy of holies of the temple (cf. 11:19) for all mankind; all people shall enter and dwell from then on in the house of God. The true Israel, the eternal Covenant are reality.

4he will wipe away every tear from their eyes, and death shall be no more, neither shall there be mourning nor crying nor pain, for the former things have passed away.

If God is truly and really to become an immediate experience for man, then all things which would impair the fulfillment of such blessedness are thereby excluded. The old type of human existence which through the curse of sin was marked by much tribulation and suffering, pain and mourning, want and death has for ever vanished with the old world (cf. 7:16).

5And he who sat upon the throne said, Behold I make all things new. Also he said, Write this for these words are trustworthy and true.

A second speaker continues with the exposition, it is God himself. As a matter of fact, this is the first and only place that Revelation lets God speak directly. The first word of God in the Bible is: "Let there be . . ." (Gen. 1:3); here his last word is recorded; it repeats the first in that it completes what was called into being by the first: "Behold, I make all things new."

God solemnly vouches for this word of consummation and commands the Seer to put this guarantee in writing. The fulfillment of his first word through this last one establishes in fact the longed for paradise on earth; in the end there will be a perfect and happy world. And it will one day show not only God's promises to be true but also God as God.

⁶ᵃAnd he said to me, It is done! I am the Alpha and the Omega, the beginning and end.

When God speaks, something happens; his word is deed (cf. Is. 55:11). Hence quite literally translated this text says: "They have happened," namely, the words whose trustworthiness had just been guaranteed. Just as in the first creation (Gen. 1:3b, 6b, etc.), the word of God will happen also in the new creation. In him, the eternal being, the beginning and end of the world are not separated in time, as creator he is at the same time its consummator; he is there at its beginning and he himself is its goal; figuratively, this fact is again expressed and made memorable by the A-O formula (cf.1:8).

⁶ᵇTo the thirsty I will give water without price from the fountain of the water of life. ⁷He who conquers shall have this heritage, and I will be his God and he shall be my son. ⁸But as for the cowardly, the faithless; the polluted, as for the murderers, sorcerers, idolaters, and all liars, their lot shall be in the lake that burns with fire and brimstone, which is the second death.

The final destiny of creation, the new world, is in conclusion turned into something for each person. He who wishes to belong to it must never lose his longing for it. The motive of Christian hope survives the periods of thirst without succumbing to the temptation of slaking the thirst for fortune and happiness at the fountains of the world. The longing of the human heart will be satisfied only in the consummation which is still concealed but will definitely come (cf. 7:17). "Without price," that is, as a

free gift of God, will the perfect final state be bestowed on him
who attains it; no one can, strictly speaking, earn it.

And yet it depends on the personal effort of the individual;
only he who has successfully battled through the ordeals of a
life of faith brings with him the precondition of finding in the
blessed communion with God the fulfillment of his being. Just
as at the end of every one of the seven letters, so here in the
prologue to the last vision we have a victor-text (cf. 2:7); here
as there it is meant as an urgent exhortation. The victor-texts
of the letters promise unchangeably the blessed consummation in
traditional images; here it happens with the image of an in-
heritance passed from father to son. God adopts him who
perseveres as a son and makes him the heir of his entire possessions.

A threat, addressed to the failures, concludes God's words; it
proclaims the fate of those who instead of achieving victory allow
themselves to succumb to a cowardly defeat. Various possibilities
of failure are listed in the manner of a catalogue of vices which
holds no claim to completeness. At the top we have the cowards
and the faithless; such who broke faith with God through a
fearful or unprincipled compliance and those who out of a
spiritual pride would not submit to God. The other moral lapses
mentioned here are summarized at the end in one key word,
" liars." Falseness in mind, word, and deed betrays a spiritual
affinity to the " father of lies " (Jn. 8:44). The promise of eternal
life is once more underlined with the contrasting threat of
eternal death. As a warning, this threat appears twice more in
the following (21:27; 22:15).

The Vision of the Consummated Creation
(21 : 9—22 : 5)

The description of the consummated creation must also be content with means of illustration found in human experience of this world; with these the Seer attempts to communicate a picture which although only analogical is nevertheless to some extent concrete and impressive. In three colorful images—the external features of the new Jerusalem (21:5–21a), internal features of the city (21:21b–27), the new paradise (22:1–5)—the happy final state of the world and mankind is unfolded. The last exposition of Revelation is the most long-drawn out in the book; one gets the impression that the Seer can hardly tear himself away from this glorious final picture of peace, joy, and happiness from whence a transfiguring light of hope also falls on the visions of horror depicted earlier. The portrayal once more makes extensive use of themes from the Old Testament prophetic glimpse of the future, especially from Ezekiel and Isaiah.

In its formal construction the vision is modeled on that of the world capital Babylon.

The New Jerusalem (21 : 9–27)

⁹*Then came one of the seven angels who had the seven bowls full of the seven last plagues, and spoke to me, saying, Come, I will show you the Bride, the wife of the Lamb.* ¹⁰*And in spirit he carried me away to a great, high mountain, and showed me the holy city Jerusalem coming down out of heaven from God, . . .*

The introduction partially tallies word for word with the one of 17:1–3. Again it is one of the seven bowl angels which here as there imparts the vision to John in an experience of rapture.

There we had the wilderness, here it is a high mountain from which the complete fulfillment of this Old Testament image is shown the Seer, just as long ago Moses was shown the promised land (Deut. 32:40). There it was the harlot on the beast, the symbol of apostasy from God and his Messiah, here it is the bride which the Lamb has fetched for the marriage feast, symbol of the most intimate communion between Christ and his Church (cf. 19:7f.); here the chosen one, there the rejected one. There, in conclusion, the harlot was interpreted to symbolize the " great city " of the antichrist (17:18), here the bride is equated with the " holy city Jerusalem."

[11]. . . *having the glory of God, its radiance like a most rare jewel, like a jasper, clear as crystal.*

The image of the bride from now on recedes behind that of the city which John is shown now, as was Ezekiel before him (Ezek. 40:2ff.). The old Jerusalem, the city, in whose temple God was present to his chosen people, is here translated entirely into the spiritual sphere to allegorize the eternal transfigured existence of redeemed mankind to whom God now reveals himself as he is.

Directly in the first sentence the main fact is named; the most proper and essential feature of the city is stressed: God's glory dwells in it; it belongs essentially to it and not like in Ezekiel where it only enters it (cf. Ezek. 43:2–5). The heaven of God is the experience of God's glory.

The total impression of the city, quite saturated with the glory of God's essence, is the same as that of the appearance of God himself (cf. 4:3); hence in both instances the means of illustration is the same: the diamond sparkling in all the colors of sunlight (cf. 4:3).

[12]*It had a great, high wall, with twelve gates, and at the gates*

twelve angels, and on the gates the names of the twelve tribes of the sons of Israel were inscribed; [13]*on the east three gates, on the north three gates, on the south three gates, and on the west three gates.* [14]*And the wall of the city had twelve foundations, and on them the names of the twelve apostles of the Lamb.*

The proper subject of the image having been defined and the focal point of the entire vision established, to deepen the impression the framework of the whole can now be described. Just as in former days the festive pilgrim approaching the holy city saw Jerusalem from afar as a single and massive bastion in the garland of its walls, battlements, and strong gates, so does John see the new Jerusalem first from afar, as it were, and begins to describe it from the outside.

First the wall attracts attention; it gives the impression of a closed unity within as well as seclusion from the outside; it divorces the inside from the outside (cf. 21:27 and 22:15). Towards the four points of the compass (four = the symbolic number of the cosmos) it is in each instance broken through by three gates (three = the symbolic number of divinity). Above the twelve doors (twelve = the symbolic number for the consummation of salvation history) twelve angels stand like sentinels (cf. Is. 62:6). But the walls no longer have the task of protecting the inhabitants from enemies as with cities of the " first earth." The new Jerusalem is a city of open gates (cf. 21:25); they invite one to enter the blazing glory which shines far afield as a promise and enjoy the blessedness of meeting the living God.

As in Ezekiel (Ezek. 48:31–34) the name of one of the twelve tribes of Israel is on every gate, but on the twelve foundations, which bear the walls and hold them together, the names of the twelve apostles of Christ (cf. Mt. 10:2; Eph. 2:20). The unity of the Old Testament and New Testament people of God is once again made quite clear (cf. 7:4–8; 12:6); moreover, the number twelve also stresses that in this city all the salvific promises of Israel, which the Church has inherited, have been fulfilled.

¹⁵And he who talked to me had a measuring rod of gold to measure the city and its gates and walls. ¹⁶The city lies four-square, its length the same as its breadth; and he measured the city with his rod, twelve thousand stadia; its length and breadth and height are equal. ¹⁷He also measured its wall, a hundred and forty-four cubits by a man's measure, that is, an angel's.

The basic number twelve is repeated also in the measurements which are evidently given to give an impression of the shape and size of the " holy city Jerusalem " (v. 10). The difficulties which, however, result if one tries with the aid of these measurements to imagine it spatially are sufficient indication that the reporter is not concerned with the picture as such but that its symbolic content alone is of significance for him.

The measuring here serves quite a different purpose to the one described in 11:1. In contrast with the latter it is here under-taken with a measuring rod suitable (" gold ") for heaven (cf. v. 18). But since it is his concern to give people on earth an idea of this transcendental reality, the angel must, as it is expressly noted, make use of measurements which are used among men; that means at the same time that the supernatural reality cannot be suitably represented by these means.

The city is constructed as a square; besides this, it is also as high as it is wide, hence it has the shape of a cube, as was also the case with the holy of holies in the tabernacle and later in the temple (square and cube were regarded in antiquity as symbols of perfection). The similarity with the holy of holies is sig-nificant; the Seer describes here the archetype and the con-summation of what in the temple of Israel existed only as an imitation and at the same time a promise, namely, the actual dwelling-place of God and his immediate presence among his people, through which the old salvific promises have now been completely fulfilled.

The recorded measurement of twelve thousand stadia (1 stadia = 192 m. or 630 ft.) would result in a cube of colossal proportions (about 2400 km., or nearly 1500 miles, high and wide); this aims to indicate not only the absolute proportionality and perfection ("twelve") but also the immeasurability ("thousand") of the new reality in which God himself is "all in all" (cf. 1 Cor. 15:28). The measurement of the height of the wall also contains the symbolic twelve squared; hence also the wall is in itself complete and appropriately adapted to the whole; its height is in comparison with the townscape so insignificantly small (70 m., 229 ft.) that it would appear improbable in relation to the entire picture and for the observer almost unrecognizable at a distance. And yet it is precisely the wall which was described in such great detail (vv. 12-14) and later attention is once more focused on it (vv. 18-21a); accordingly, the Seer appears to allot to it a special significance, especially since the purpose of protection, which city walls had at that time, is no longer applicable (cf. vv. 12-14). The description so far lets one conjecture that he sees in it something like the eternalized form of the historical people of God's salvation, that, therefore, the preliminary realization of the kingdom of God on earth in the old and new Covenant remains somehow visible in its consummated state. History does not sink into eternity without a trace; realities which evolved historically will eternally bear the imprint which shows this and which also proclaims the significance which accrued to them in history or was intended for them.

¹⁸The wall was built of jasper, while the city was pure gold, clear as glass. ¹⁹The foundations of the wall of the city were adorned with every jewel; the first was jasper, the second sapphire, the

third agate, the fourth emerald, [20]the fifth onyx, the sixth carnelian, the seventh chrysolite, the eighth beryl, the ninth topaz, the tenth chrysoprase, the eleventh jacinth, the twelfth amethyst. [21a]And the twelve gates were twelve pearls, each of the gates made of a single pearl, . . .

After the description of the overall aspect of the city and the annotation of the measurements, the building material is now mentioned of which city and wall are made (cf. Is. 54:11f.; Tob. 13:17). The city consists of pure gold and the wall of "jasper," very likely the precious stone called diamond nowadays.

Only the most beautiful and most valuable materials of the earth are of use to give us some idea of the abundance of heavenly glory. That even these valuable building materials do not adaquately reflect what John sees and would like to describe is expressed by the fact that he must add to the gold of heaven a property which it does not possess on earth: it shines in itself so pure that it is like transparent glass. The preciousness and beauty of the new Jerusalem is as unimaginable as its size.

Once again the wall receives special attention (cf. vv. 12–14). The material out of which the already mentioned foundations of the wall (v. 14) are made, is especially valuable. Every single stone consists of a great jewel and all twelve are different in their way. Since the names of jewels in those days do not tally with ours, the special colors and their possible symbolism remain uncertain. However, the enumeration of so many different stones is intended to give us an idea in what kind of iridescent, resplendent glory the heaven of God has enveloped the world.

Every city gate consists of a single wonderful pearl which indicates how much more precious the interior must be if even the entrance is so incomparably beautifully and preciously constructed.

To explain the twelve jewels, which are noted as the foundations of the wall, one usually refers to the gilded breastplace of the highpriest which was decorated with twelve jewels bearing the names of the twelve tribes of Israel (cf. Ex. 28:17–21; 39: 10–13). It is quite possible that in making the list the Seer had this most distinguished piece of liturgical clothing of the old Covenant in mind, the more so as in the description of the wall earlier on we found the twelve tribes (v. 12) beside the twelve apostles (v. 14). Also the fact that the " holy city " (v. 10) is built in the shape of the holy of holies (cf. v. 16) and is the place of God's presence in its entirety (cf. v. 22) leads one to assume that in the vision of the new Jerusalem still further symbolic material from the temple cult had been tacitly utilized. The allusion to the priestly function of the people of God, which would be implied in the reference to the breastplate of the highpriest, would confirm the conjecture expressed above concerning the total symbolic meaning of the wall.

[21b] . . . *and the street of the city was pure gold, transparent as glass.* [22]*And I saw no temple in the city, for its temple is the Lord God Almighty and the Lamb.* [23]*And the city has no need of sun or moon to shine upon it, for the glory of God is its light, and its lamp is the Lamb.*

From the externals, the description now moves to the inside of the city. The street which John sees beginning inside the gate is paved with the same material as that out of which the whole city is made.

The city center of the old Jerusalem consisted of the great temple installation; in the new Jerusalem there is no temple. For it came into existence in that God's heaven came down to the new earth; if God is present on earth as he is in heaven, the temple becomes superfluous, as in the old Jerusalem it was but the promise of what now has come to pass in the new Jerusalem; when what was symbolized has become reality, the symbol ceases to exist. Now the entire city is the " dwelling of God with men " (21:3), God and Christ are present in it everywhere and immediately and no longer only in symbolic signs as in the first temple. He who enters the new Jerusalem does not as in the " holy of holies " of the old temple stand before God; here he stands in him, he is completely surrounded by him, he lives in him.

Where the glory of God flares up, which also radiates from the Lamb, all earthly light fades. Sun and moon were created by God to give the old earth light (cf. Gen. 1:15); they have become superfluous because the eternal light of the everlasting presence of God illumines the new Jerusalem. Their second function of dividing day from night (Gen. 1:14) has also fallen away; from now on there is eternal day, because the glory of God can neither decrease nor increase; it abhors any kind of obscuration, nor does it permit any trace of darkness (cf. 1 Jn. 1:5). " The Lamb " which had unceasingly introduced itself to men as the " light of the world " now reveals to those who see it in glory why it could assert this of itself and what this assertion means fundamentally. If it has equally said to those who followed it: " You are the light of the world " (Mt. 5:14), then this means that it wishes to shine in the world through them. This is only possible to him who becomes like Christ in his person, word, and deed. In the measure in which Christ has been formed in him he will in heaven be resplendent in that light which is Christ.

[24]By its light shall the nations walk; and the kings of the earth shall bring their glory into it, [25]and its gates shall never shut by day—and there shall be no night there; [26]they shall bring into it the glory and the honor of the nations. [27]But nothing unclean

shall enter it, nor anyone who practices abomination or false-
hood, but only those who are written in the Lamb's book of life.

Because in the new Jerusalem there is uninterrupted daylight,
its city gates, shut at night in the old Jerusalem, remain constantly open to admission. The prophets had foretold the attrac-
tion of its iridescent beauty (cf. Is. 60 : 1–22); they had in spirit
foreseen how the nations of the earth draw near from all sides
in order to walk and be in the glorious light of the city of God
(cf. Is. 2 : 2–4; 60 : 3; Agg. 2 : 6–9). Misunderstandings between
nations have now become impossible because in the clarity of
divine light the unclouded truth and all reality is revealed as it
is; now there is eternal peace (cf. Is. 2 : 4; Agg. 2 : 9).

The nations of the earth no longer envy one another the power
and possessions each has; for all bring with them their wealth
and precious objects to lay them in homage at the feet of their
God. National greatness no longer produces egotistical national
pride; it is now dedicated unreservedly to the glory of God.
With unshakable and most fervent conviction, the kings of the
earth bow down as servants before the Almighty; united in this
service they remain eternally in harmony with one another. In
God all nations have found themselves; they have learned to
respect and value one another in their idiosyncrasies; with the
insight that they owe what they are and have to the greatness
and goodness of God, and partially also to the achievements of
others, they are grateful to God and grateful to one another and
in the love of God a selfless and pure love of each other is per-
fected. In this picture, so over-exposed to the splendor of heaven
that the light of the sun fades in it, all real values of this world
and all genuine achievements of mankind which have been
wrought in the fulfillment of the creator's charge to subdue the
earth (cf. Gen. 1 : 28) acquire eternal durability. What was said
of the individual who sees his goal in God and finds his happi-

ness in him—" their deeds follow them " (14:13)—is repeated here in general terms and extended to the human community, its individual groups and associations which now united in a single body as one mankind stand before God's throne. In the world picture of divine revelation there is no trace of genuine dualism, hence there is no pessimism either; together with the omnipotence of God the uniqueness and unity of God the creator and consummator remain perceptible throughout. Consequently, even in the images of destruction which are seen and willed as processes of purification from the viewpoint of the final goal, we find perhaps a note of regret (cf. 18:21–24) but never one of nihilistic triumph. Revelation's sympathy with culture and mankind is originally tied to its idea of God and results therefrom as a necessary consequence.

Everything that is genuine, good, and beautiful on earth will be eternalized in God's heaven. Genuine cultural achievements also have their eschatological significance. As in case of the human body, there is also a resurrection for " the glory of the nations," whereby all works share in the consummation of him who produced them. All who in God's name committed themselves to true values, and dispensed them through their life's work will in God and with God enjoy the harvest of wealth and beauty, not least so because they had a share in this yield through personal commitment; purified and transfigured, the achievements of mankind acquire in the new consummated creation everlasting durability.

Finally, we look at the inhabitants of the new Jerusalem; this is another occasion for the Seer in this context to call to mind the guideline of the judgment (cf. 20:12) and to repeat the threat from v. 8; but now after this heartwarming vision its sense has modified to an encouraging exhortation to decide for this eternity with a happy heart and in time.

The New Paradise (22 : 1–5)

This section is formally separated from the previous one by an
introduction ("Then he showed me"). There is also a modifica-
tion in the image; the image of the city is complemented by the
image of paradise. The two then merge into one and so the
follow-up argument comes into play: in the descent of the new
Jerusalem the lost paradise is once more given back to earth in
a consummated form. The perspective of salvation history has
widened to embrace creation history.

The first book of the Bible began with paradise which in-
augurated the history of God with mankind; with paradise the
last book of the Bible concludes whereby this history flows into
a new happy beginning without fixed limits; the final time and
the starting time correspond. The city of God, till now mainly
characterized as the city of eternal light, is with the help of the
idea of paradise also portrayed as the city of eternal life.

¹*Then he showed me the river of the water of life, bright as
crystal, flowing from the throne of God and of the Lamb . . .*

John sees the river of life spring from the "throne of God and
of the Lamb"; the primary source of eternal life is once more
through "the Lamb as though slain" accessible to mankind.
Especially for the oriental, water and life are inseparably connected; for where he sees water there is an abundance of growth;
where it is lacking there is wilderness. The fusion of the image
of a river of paradise (Gen. 2: 10–14) with the prophetic promise
of a spring of water in the temple of the final time (Ezek. 47:
1–12; Jn. 4:18; Zech. 14:8) aims to impress upon the mind the
inexhaustible fullness of vitality which God bestows on his
creation when he now, having prepared for it through redemption, brings it to its consummation.

² . . . *through the middle of the street of the city; also, on either side of the river, the tree of life with its twelve kinds of fruit, yielding its fruit each month; and the leaves of the tree were for the healing of the nations.* ³ª*There shall no more be anything accursed,* . . .

The image of the tree of life standing in the center (Gen. 2:3; 3:22) also has its source in paradise (cf. 2:7; 22:14, 19). The information given here does not permit one to determine the exact position of the tree of life. It seems that John does not have a single tree in mind like in the story of paradise. Rather, like Ezekiel, whose account he uses as a model down to the wording itself (cf. Ezek. 47:7, 12), he pictures it as an entire avenue of trees which grow along both sides of the river. The evergreen trees bear fruit uninterruptedly, that is to say, the supply of the food of immortality is never exhausted by the inhabitants of the new paradise. A second trait, that their leaves possess healing powers, is borrowed directly from Ezekiel (cf. Ezek. 47:12) and can in this context be valid only in the limited sense that all newly arrived people find healing from all infirmity and receive the gift of preservation of their new life from all mortal threat. For illness and death, consequences of the curse of sin, can no longer be there (cf. 21:4). In fact, nothing accursed is there anymore (cf. Zech. 14:11) since the cause of all evil, Satan, remains excluded from the new world for all eternity (cf. 20:10).

³ᵇ . . . *but the throne of God and the Lamb shall be in it, and his servants shall worship him;* ⁴*they shall see his face, and his name will be on their foreheads.* ⁵*And night shall be no more; they need no light of lamp or sun, for the Lord God will be their light, and they shall reign for ever and ever.*

The visions of the future ("what is to take place hereafter,"
1:19) began with the throne vision (4:1—5:14). They now end
at the "throne of God and of the Lamb." The heaven of God
and the world of mankind had been two separate realities; they
have now once again become one. A new fall into sin, as in the
first paradise, is for ever excluded.

Marked as the image and possession of God (cf. 3:12; 14:1),
new mankind, united with the heavenly hosts, stands in loyal
service before the face of the Most High; precisely for that
reason does he give them a share in his sovereignty (cf. 1:6;
3:21; 5:10). In this respect, too, what has been foreshadowed in
the first paradise, but remained unsuccessful through the sin of
man, is in the new paradise fully and completely fulfilled (cf.
Gen. 1:28f.; 2:15–17; 3:1–7, 23f.).

Those who stand before the throne of God see God as he is
(cf. Mt. 5:8; 1 Cor. 12:12; 1 Jn. 3:2), that is the essence of their
happiness. In the eternal light of God's glory they have found
eternal life. Only now the creature, man, is complete in everything that he was endowed with. The immediate and eternal
living communion with God his creator and redeemer alone
gives his nature the fulfillment decreed for it. God, the Lord
who has created the first paradise and has restored it more
magnificent and beautiful in the new is now experienced by the
blessed in all eternity as their A and O, their beginning and
consummation.

With this eternal future of mankind a true future is also
conferred on all that belongs to man's world; the transfiguration
embraces the entire creation of God; the new heaven and the
new earth (cf. 21:1) are realized when, and in that, God becomes
"everything to everyone" (cf. 1 Cor. 15:28); this future of God
establishes and determines the eternal future of the universe.

EPILOGUE (22:6–21)

Threefold Testimony to the
Book of Revelation (22:6–9)

*⁶And he said to me, These words are trustworthy and true. And
the Lord, the God of the spirits of the prophets, has sent his
angel to show his servants what must soon take place.*

The main concern of the epilogue is to testify to the absolute
trustworthiness of the revelation contained in the book. This
had already been done earlier and partly with the same words
as here (cf. 19:9; 21:5). The confirmation there was meant for
specific statements; here it refers to the whole book and consequently receives a more solemn and impressive formulation.

The first testimony is given by the angel who showed John
the last vision: that it refers beyond this to include the total
content is adequately indicated by the almost word for word
reference of the text to the first sentence of Revelation (cf.
1:1–3). It establishes trustworthiness with the indication that
the revelation comes from God himself (cf. 1:1). As the Lord of
"the spirits of the prophets" (cf. 1 Cor. 14:32), God inspires
those whom he wishes to take into his service as prophets with
what he wants to have made known. The phrase: "what must
soon take place" announced the theme of the book in the introduction (1:1), and with the same words its content is summarized in the epilogue.

*⁷And behold, I am coming soon. Blessed is he who keeps the
words of the prophecy of this book.*

The two attestations come from Christ. He repeats thereby the theme announced in the previous verse with the clarifying assurance that it is he himself who is coming soon (cf. 2 : 16; 3 : 11); this announcement is twice more confirmed in the following (vv. 12 and 20). It expresses, depending on the context, threat (cf. 2 : 16; 3 : 11), urgent exhortation (cf. 16 : 15), and also encouragement. The pastoral concern of Revelation to conjure up loyalty and give courage for the time of persecution with the pointer to the outcome of all history once more makes itself felt at the end with special urgency. A beatitude which echoes the first beatitude of the book (1 : 3) confirms the appeal to all to take the revealed truths seriously and live by them.

8I John am he who heard and saw these things. And when I heard and saw them I fell down to worship at the feet of the angel who showed them to me; 9but he said to me, You must not do that! I am a fellow servant with you and your brethren the prophets, and with those who keep the words of this book. Worship God.

In third place the author himself vouches for the genuineness of the revelation contained in his book. He was an eye- and ear-witness of it all and recorded it at Christ's command (cf. 1 : 11). Again he calls himself simply John (cf. 1 : 9); he is well known and known as trustworthy.

Nevertheless, he adds a personal testimony issued for him by the angel of revelation. When, as once before (cf. 19 : 10), overcome by the majesty of his prophetic calling and deeply impressed by the great significance for the distressed Church of the revelation imparted to him, he intends to worship the angel, the ambassador of God in warding him off expressly confirms his prophetic calling and at the same time the contents of his writing as a true prophecy for the second time (cf. v. 6).

Just as the angels and the chosen prophets glorify God by a loyal service, so do those who keep to the guide-lines of the prophetic propagation contained in the book; as servants of God they are thus in the same class as the angels and his prophets.

The Command to Publish the Revelation; Final Admonition of Christ (22:10–16)

[10]*And he said to me, Do not seal up the words of the prophecy of this book, for the time is near.*

In contrast with the prophet Daniel, who was forbidden to publish his visions (cf. Dan. 8:26; 12:49), John receives the command to make his known immediately. The difference in the command is based on the fact that Daniel's prophecies referred to a later time (cf. Dan. 8:26), that is, the " final time " which had not yet arrived (cf. Dan. 12:49). The visions of John, however, are important for the contemporary Church for her orientation and strengthening. The message which John received and passes on uncovers the true history behind world events; it is prophecy.

As distinct from the prophet, the historian finds in the past clues and laws which help him to understand the present. In contrast, the prophet explains the present with the aid of the future by taking into account the final goal of the historical process. The final goal of all history has come to light in the history of Jesus Christ. The special feature of his history is that it happened " once for all " (cf. Rom. 6:10; Heb. 7:27; 9:12; 10:10); with it something absolutely new and enduring began for this world-time; the phenomenon of Christ is an anticipatory happening in which the absolute future was anticipated.

In the history of Christ, therefore, the true meaning of all history was disclosed. With the death and resurrection of Jesus the end of the old and the beginning of the new world was fixed; with the transfigured Christ the eternal future of creation in the consummated sovereignty of God became visible in world-time for the first time and entered it forever; from then on this future of God already had a provisional bearing on world history till at the return of the transfigured Lord it is consummated and makes its full appearance even externally.

Because of this knowledge of the absolute future of God, which is absolutely assured to mankind in the happening of Christ, Christian prophecy knows how to interpret the present. All the pictorial accounts of Revelation sought to make the world process transparent with regard to this concealed reality, its true history.

[11]*Let the evildoer still do evil, and the filthy still be filthy, and the righteous still do right, and the holy still be holy.*

The final time has begun with the life of Jesus Christ. The separation of spirits is, therefore, already taking place; the fronts of good and evil are lining themselves up clearly opposite each other. This ascertainment is expressed as an imperative in order to stress with this literary trope in addition the freedom of choice, a guarantee of free will.

The human being realizes himself as a being who plans and builds his own future; by virtue of his freedom he executes actions in the present which anticipate his future. Consequently, he will one day stand before God's judgment seat as the person he has made himself; the judgment only fixes the final point; it eternalizes the shape everyone has acquired for himself. The wicked do not enter the eternal glory of God's kingdom because those " who do not want to be in there cannot be in there."

[12]Behold I am coming soon, bringing my recompense, to repay everyone for what he has done.

When Christ in this context repeats the announcement of his imminent advent, it takes the form of a threat of judgment. Within a short time the good as well as the wicked will experience him as judge who repays everyone, rewarding or punishing according to his life's work (cf. 2:23; 20:11f.).

[13]I am the Alpha and the Omega, the first and the last, the beginning and the end.

Christ will appear at the judgment in his divine glory and pronounce judgment with full divine authority. The divine titles of majesty which are added here to establish this (cf. 1:8; 21:6) were already ascribed to him earlier on (cf. 1:17; 2:8). These now establish clearly why judgment can be ascribed equally to Christ (22:12) as to God (20:11).

[14]Blessed are those who wash their robes, that they may have the right to the tree of life and that they may enter the city by the gates. [15]Outside are the dogs and sorcerers and fornicators and murderers and idolaters, and everyone who loves and practices falsehood.

The seventh and last beatitude of Revelation modifies the warning of judgment to a positive admonition to be ready for it, or, to get ready for it. For eternal happiness is at stake which was so impressively described in the twofold image of the new Jerusalem (21:9–27) and the return of paradise (22:1–5). A formal right to it belongs to those who appropriate to themselves in faith and deed the fruit of Christ's vicarious death of atonement (cf. 7:14). To make the seriousness of this decision clear

as day, an anticipated judgment of perdition follows on all who
by their own fault miss the road to the holy city Jerusalem and
into paradise. Those who remain outside are again recorded
in a so-called catalogue of vices which essentially tallies with the
one in 21:8. Instead of the "polluted" we have here the
"dogs"; even to this day dog is a common and severe insult
in the Orient; in Scripture the dog appears as an archetype of
uncleanliness (cf. Mt. 7:6; 2 Pet. 2:22). Moreover, the "liars"
are here more precisely characterized as those who in mind and
deed are mendacious.

¹⁶*I Jesus have sent my angel to you with this testimony for the
churches. I am the root and the offspring of David, the bright
morning star.*

Two sparse I-sentences conclude the words of Jesus. They link
the end of the book with the beginning. Jesus testifies to himself
here as the author of the revelation contained in the book (cf.
1:1; 22:6) intended for the seven churches (cf. 1:11). This
personal testimony is an indirect repetition of the authentication
in v. 7. When the angel of revelation declares in v. 6 that God
had sent him, but here Christ declares himself the sender, then
this apparent contradiction is resolved in the same manner as
the other with regard to the final judgment (cf. v. 13).

The second personal testimony establishes the first by recalling
to mind the position of Jesus in salvation history in the light of
Old Testament prophecies. Jesus had already introduced himself
earlier on (cf. 5:5) as the "root of David" (cf. Is. 11:1),
meaning, shoot from the root of David, that is, Son of David.
He is besides also the "offspring of David," that is, his descen-
dant who has realized all the Messianic promises which God had
made to David; the representative of David's tribe who is not
only David's Son but also David's Lord (cf. 22:41–45 par.), the

Messiah-king (cf. 2 Sam. 7:16), the " King of kings " (cf. 17:14; 19:16). The third self-characterization, morning star, fits in with this (cf. 2:28). It very probably relies on the prophecy of Balaam (Num. 24:17) which was already in Judaism demonstrably interpreted messianically with reference to the world sovereignty of the Messiah.

Longing for the Imminent Coming of Christ; Warning against Falsification of the Recorded Revelation; Final Greeting (22:17–21)

[17]The Spirit and the Bride say, Come. And let him who hears say, Come. And let him who is thirsty come, let him who desires take the water of life without price.

So far in the epilogue we have heard words of Christ, words of the angel of revelation and words of the Seer; here two more voices are added, those of the Spirit and of the Bride. The Bride has already appeared as a symbol of the Church (19:7f.; 21:2, 9), indeed, of the Church in heaven and the Church on earth. The Church which has arrived at its goal at the throne of the sovereign Lord and the earthly Church which is on the way to this goal are both united in longing and in prayer for the consummation of God's kingdom. Also the Spirit who spoke to the Church (cf. 2:7, 11 etc.) and spoke in the prophetic words of the Seer (cf. v. 6), makes the plea of the Church entirely his own. The promise of Christ has granted his Church on earth the Holy Spirit as Counsellor (Jn. 14:16) who according to the words of the Apostle Paul takes on human weakness and intercedes in the proper manner for the interests of the faithful before God (cf. Rom. 8:26f.). This Holy Spirit, together with the bridal Church, calls to Christ: Come! All who hear this call to prayer of the Spirit at the reading of the text during assembly for divine service are called upon to join in this prayer.

To all who await with longing the advent of their Lord, a word of comfort is uttered: even in the present he will permit them, the redeemed, to drink from the spring of eternal life (cf. Is. 53:1; Jn. 7:37-39) and, indeed, " without price " (cf. 21:6).

[18]*I warn everyone who hears the words of the prophecy of this book: if anyone adds to them, God will add to him the plagues described in this book,* [19]*and if anyone takes away from the words of the book of this prophecy, God will take away his share in the tree of life and in the holy city which are described in this book.*

Just as the law of the old Covenant was secured against additions and deletion (cf. Deut. 4:2; 13:1), so in conclusion John also secures the revelation he was commanded to write down from any such falsification. Anyone who acts against this will in line with the law of recompense of equal kind and equal measure (*ius talionis*) draw the plagues on himself which are recorded in the writing, or lose his share in the salvation promised in it. John, therefore, makes the same claim for his writing as the Old Testament law made for itself; indirectly, Revelation is thereby attested once more as the word of God.

[20]*He who testifies to these things says, Surely I am coming soon. Amen. Come, Lord Jesus!*

The last word of the book of Revelation is uttered by Jesus. He answers the prayer which the Bride in the Holy Spirit has addressed to him for the third time in this epilogue with the assurance that he will come soon. The waiting Bride, the

Church, answers him with Amen and adds once more her petition with the prayer cry handed down in Aramaic from the liturgy of the infant Church and here translated into Greek: Maranatha, Come, Lord Jesus! (cf. 1 Cor. 16:22; Teaching of the Twelve Apostles 10:6). He who awaits the coming Lord with the certainty of faith and truly gladdens his life with this hope, and with loving desire longs and prays for the consummation of God's kingdom ("thy kingdom come") has grasped the message of the last book of God's revelation and made it his own.

[21]*The grace of the Lord Jesus be with all [the saints. Amen].*

Just as in the beginning of the book there was a greeting similar to those we find in the Letters of the Apostles (cf. 1:4-6), so this writing, as it was intended to be read at divine service, ends like those letters with a greeting; it is a benediction which desires for all the grace of Jesus their exalted Lord, so that they might reach the goal described in Revelation which, indeed, will cost effort, but is indescribably glorious.

Some manuscripts have the addition "saints" after "all"; this will have its source in the title which Paul confers on the faithful in his epistolatory addresses. The equally belated additional final Amen is the liturgical acclamation with which the faithful during divine service answered affirmatively to a vocal prayer or a Scriptural reading.